HENRY APPLETON BOY HERO AND THE BURGESS GANG

HENRY APPLETON
BOY HERO
AND THE BURGESS GANG

A JOHNNY SLICK NOVEL

BY JOHN EVAN HARRIS
AUTHOR OF *THE PHYSICIAN'S GUN*

ILLUSTRATED BY CHARLES CUMMING
COVER ILLUSTRATION BY LAURA KING

ROIALL EMERALD PUBLISHERS

Fictionally originally published in the USA in 1874

First published in New Zealand 2023

Roiall Emerald Publishers, Level 2, 9 St Mary's Road, St Mary's Bay, Auckland 1011, Aotearoa New Zealand. PO Box 147 611 Ponsonby, Auckland 1144, New Zealand.

Author website: www.johnevanharris.com
Publisher website: www.boyfellinpond.com

978-0-473-66565-4 (Paperback)
978-0-473-66567-8 (EPUB)

TO THE 21st CENTURY READER

Henry Appleton, Boy Hero was fictionally written in 1874, and much has changed since then – notably society's attitudes to race relations, gender equality, capital punishment and other issues which feature in the book. Please keep this in mind when reading the words of Johnny Slick, who was a product of his time. No attempt has been made to censor or abridge his writing, and some passages may offend.

CONTENTS

PUBLISHER'S NOTE

A note from Roiall Emerald Publishers

Henry Appleton, Boy Hero, and the Burgess Gang

The author Johnny Slick was always on the lookout for inspiration for his next dime novel. While on a lecture tour of New Zealand in 1866, and staying in Nelson, he met the young Henry Appleton, who at that stage was an aspiring writer himself. Appleton became embroiled with the Burgess gang, who later committed the infamous Maungatapu Murders.

Slick extended his stay in New Zealand in order to cover the trial of the murderers, and their execution, for newspapers in the United States. He asked Henry for permission to write a full account of the young man's encounters with the gang, and admitted later that Henry declined. However it is evident from the contents of this book that Henry later relented to a certain extent and gave Slick an interview. This forms the basis of the early childhood stories which appear in this novel.

Appleton went on to train as a physician, before going into practice in Nelson. He took his wife and young son to America a few years later, and Slick was proud to introduce the young doctor and his family to the president at the time.

Henry Appleton, Boy Hero was by no means the last book Johnny Slick penned. A prolific author, he produced at least a dozen more novels, several of them set in New Zealand.

ABOUT JOHNNY SLICK

Little is known about the American novelist Johnny Slick. He claimed to be a prolific writer, and often boasted about it. But it is very unlikely he penned more books than his contemporary Colonel E Z C Judson. (Under the nom de plume Ned Buntline, Judson is reputed to have written some 300 dime novels, including *Buffalo Bill and his adventures in the West.*) This novel, *Henry Appleton Boy Hero*, is one of the few which can reliably be attributed to Slick, although Henry Appleton was in no doubt that Slick was the author of *Shootout at Dead Man's Creek.*

It is likely Slick was born around 1820 in Oklahoma, but the place and date of his death are unknown. We know he was in New Zealand in 1866, because of his writings about the Burgess Gang, and some believe he may have died here. But he was back in the United States in 1874, when he published his novel *Henry Appleton, Boy Hero.*

Slick led a colourful life, punctuated by frequent brushes with the law, and if he is to be believed he was often in the company of some of America's most famous sons. As he told Henry Appleton, he once challenged the gunslinger Wild Bill Hickok to a duel which ended farcically because both men were incapacitated by alcohol.

There is an unverified report that a gravestone was uncovered in New Zealand in the early 1900s, reading *'Here lies the famed American author Johnny Slick, who died heroically rescuing a young mother and her children from the Waikato River.'* Most likely this report is as unreliable as any of Johnny Slick's adventures. We have been unable to locate such a grave – and even if it existed, it is more than likely the inscription was drafted by the dime novelist himself.

John Evan Harris
Author of *The Physician's Gun*

ONE
DELIVERY BY STORM

An icy rain pummels the small cottage at the edge of a great forest. A dim lantern swings in the front window, and the hand painted *'Bluebell Cottage'* sign is tossed this way and that as the wind strains to wrench it off its hooks.

Look well at the young man who stands at the front door, grasping its frame as he is buffeted by the mocking wind, and peers into the darkness of the New Zealand bush. He is barely 14, but his body is already forged and hardened by this harsh country which has a special disdain for those who venture across the oceans and dare to call this home.

"Father!" he cries into the storm.

"Whoo whoo!" replies a ghostly owl in the treetops.

Behind the house, in a patch of tilled land which is

planted in various types of vegetable, is the young man's mother, thin and muscular. She wears threadbare trousers borrowed from her husband's wardrobe, rolled up and hitched with a piece of cord; and his shirt also, knotted at the waist. Her boots are a pair which no longer fit her son.

It is not far from midnight, and the moon's light is mostly blanketed by dark cloud and rain, but this woman wields a spade with ferocious intensity. Only hours ago, a runner from the goldfields brought the news that her husband is dead, and in her grief and anger she attacks the dirt that represents her hope and her despair.

"William, why?" she sobs. In London no more than four years gone, Victoria Appleton was a gentlewoman who wore fine clothes and spent her days in the society of other educated women. Now her matted hair forms a veil over her fine features, and her hands are blistered and cracked from hard labour.

"Why?" Her warm tears mingle with the icy rain-drops and her spade slices into the plants she has so carefully tended.

Hark now! Above the howl of the storm can be heard an eerie screech as if some miserable animal is in pain.

"Father!" At the front of the house Henry Appleton, for this is the young man's name, calls out again.

The animal's screech now reveals itself to be the creaking of wagon wheels.

The boy, already drenched, flings himself into the storm, slipping and sliding in the mud as he scrambles towards the trees.

The wagon appears in the mist before him as a spectre materialising from Hades. It is a narrow and battered wooden vehicle drawn by a miserable pack-horse, and lined on each side are the hooded denizens of the underworld; or so they appear to be.

"Hallo – Appletons!" cries one. He pulls back his hood, regardless of the tiny daggers of rain which stab his bearded face. "Appletons – ahoy!" This man is Hans, and he is from Germany, but that is all his comrades know. Like the rest of them, he has left behind his old life to search for gold in this far-off land. Perhaps he is the youngest son of a wealthy land owner; perhaps he killed a rival in a fight and can never return. No-one knows, and no-one cares. Tonight the guardians of the wagon are simply united in their concern for a fellow gold digger and his widow and son.

The other men drop their hoods and flick the rain from their hair. These are young men from places far away, drawn to New Zealand's goldfields by stories of adventure and great riches. They are by now more accustomed to death than they would wish to tell. They stand alert, as sentinels, having delivered their forlorn consignment.

The Appleton boy stops abruptly, confronted by the wagon's sorry cargo. He knows that beneath the water-logged oilskin, lashed down by rope bindings, is the body of his father William Appleton. He sees his father's boots, heavy with mud, protruding from the cover.

"William!" The widow runs from the cottage. She flings her thin frame against the shape of her husband's body, sobbing. Hans the bearded German wraps a powerful arm around her to support her and they drag the cart close to the cottage. He says nothing. There is nothing to say when a man hands a widow her dead husband.

"Come inside, please," says the widow. She has already stopped crying, and she knows the men will be hungry after their long trek through the storm. There is a large pot of soup simmering for them. The men remove their sodden coats and boots and step into the cottage, grateful for its warmth.

While they spoon down the soup, and the widow fusses over them and thanks them for their troubles, the boy remains outside. He offers the cart horse a bucket of water, then stands silently next to his father's shrouded body.

He is grieving, of course; the dead man is the only

father Henry has ever known. But William Appleton was not Henry's birth father, and although Henry had a happy life with William and Victoria Appleton in England, and although William was a good father and cared deeply for Henry, the boy longs to know his real father. Was he an adventurer? A writer? A lord, or a pauper?

Henry has always known that his real mother gave him up for adoption, and he accepts she must have had good cause. But he has that gnawing pain that every adopted child experiences, always wondering *why*.

These thoughts occupy Henry's mind as he stands alongside the cart. The rain continues to pepper him with icy shots, but he pays no heed. He helps the men carry his father's body into the cottage and lay it on the table. He helps them turn the cart around in the mud. And he watches as the men with the horse and cart are once more swallowed by the mist and rain.

TWO

HIS FIRST ADVENTURE

Now we turn back the pages of Henry's life. For as they say, the nature of the man can be seen in the boy. I, Johnny Slick, having been afforded the privilege of spending time with Henry Appleton, can now recount some of his earlier adventures.

Travel with me, if you will, to March 9th, 1862, a month shy of Henry's 11th birthday, when we will witness an event which gives us an early signal of Henry Appleton's heroic nature.

On this day, Henry accompanied his father to town while William Appleton visited the W. H. West Hair Dressing Saloon in Hardy Street, Nelson.

It was not a regular occurrence, because Mrs Appleton preferred that her husband stay at home and help dig the garden behind Bluebell Cottage, rather than go to what she described as "a den of iniquity". But this day she resigned herself to spending the morning without her husband and son, and bid them farewell as they set off in the old cart which their elderly horse Solomon could barely pull.

William Appleton waved a cheery goodbye, and gave his son a friendly punch on the arm.

"Just the two of us men," he said. "Just the two of us."

Henry sat head high beside him, grinning, as they juddered down the rough track towards the town.

They did not talk. His father began to hum an old English tune Henry did not recognize, and there was a faraway look in his eyes. Henry was happy to think about nothing, but simply to gaze at the shimmering trees as they passed by.

As they entered the dark forest, William Appleton stopped humming.

"Hard times," he muttered to himself. "Hard times."

"I know," said Henry in a small voice.

Henry knew his father would be thinking about his debts. They owed a lot of money to the bank, and sometimes they had nothing to eat but potatoes from their own garden.

Henry wished he could help. But he had no money, and no way to earn any money.

Then, as they came out of the forest into more open countryside, William Appleton awoke from his dream and turned to Henry.

"Henry, son ," he said. "Take the reins."

He handed the worn leather straps to the boy, and for the next few minutes Henry sat proudly in charge, firmly guiding old Solomon along the uneven track.

When they arrived in town William took back the reins. "Well done, Henry," he said. "Well done." He hitched the wagon, and disappeared into the W. H. West Hair Dressing Saloon.

Henry peered through the window at the shelves stacked with toys and well-thumbed newspapers. Signs pointed to fireworks, gun powder and shot for firearms. There was a majestic iron barber's chair with arm rests and a footrest so customers could stretch out.

A few years ago, Henry would have been taken inside to play with the toys, but he was too old for that now. He knew his father would be in there for a good two hours, chatting with friends and reading the papers, so he skipped across the muddy road and sat on the bench to watch the world go by.

Already his mind was active, as he began to draft another short story for his Wild West collection. Cowboys and Indians, gunfights, horses and cattle drives, heroes and villains...

His attention was drawn to a pair of strangers who rode up on horses which glistened with sweat. The men were clearly villains, Henry decided, and made a mental note of their features. The older man had a bushy beard and drooping hat which nearly concealed his face, but it was his eyes that marked the man. His left eye was a steely blue, but his right eye was dead and devoid of any hue.

Henry's gaze turned to the younger man, whose only interesting feature was his neatly-trimmed pencil moustache. He looked back at the older man; "Dead Eye Dick", Henry said under his breath. What a character for his next story! How could anyone with a dead eye like that be anything but a villain?

Henry's attention to detail was an asset he was keen to develop, for the sake of his writing career. He made a point of examining the men's dusty footwear – a buckle was missing from the older man's right boot – and their trousers were grubby, their jackets crumpled. Dead Eye Dick wore a filthy neckerchief which warranted no mention, but the younger man had a pleasant blue and white cravat tied neatly round his neck. Very smart, thought Henry. "Flash Freddie," he named him.

The men stopped their horses next to the hitching rail only a few yards away, and dismounted. Henry flinched as Dead Eye Dick coughed loudly and spat a large wodge of soggy tobacco into the dirt, almost at Henry's feet. The man fixed Henry with his one good eye, then turned away. Henry gulped. Were they aware he had been observing them keenly?

He made a point of bending down to tie his boot laces, and the men walked off down the road. Off to have a few drinks at one of the hotels around the corner, no doubt. Henry noted the saddlebags they each carried. He was puzzled; the way the men swung them made it obvious the bags were empty.

When the men were gone, Henry studied the horses. One stood out because of the dash of white on its chest. No other detail to memorise, except – Henry frowned. Neither man had secured the reins very tightly to the hitching rail. The reins had simply been looped across the rail, and Henry wondered if he should jump up and tie them properly. But his mother had often admonished him for poking his nose into other people's business. It would get him into big trouble one day, she warned. So he remained where he was, and turned his attention to other passers-by.

An elderly man, his back stooped, shepherded his frisky grandson across the road. Where were they off to, Henry wondered. He heard raucous laughter from inside the saloon. What jokes were they telling? Knowing his father, the jokes would be quite proper.

"Henry, laddie!" He blinked. About to enter the saloon was Constable John Nash, the Irish policeman who had arrived only recently but already seemed to know everyone in town.

"Good morning, sir," he called back.

The constable removed his military cap and stepped inside the saloon, to be greeted by a chorus of friendly calls.

Henry Appleton sometimes wondered about becoming a soldier. A life of adventure and danger was alluring, and he was sure his father would approve. But not his mother. She raised her hands in protest whenever he mentioned his Western heroes – lawmen, and the occasional bandit. And riders of the Pony Express. Some of them were only a year older than Henry himself. Thundering across the plains, chased by Indians and wolves, carrying their precious mail.

Henry began to doze, and dreamt of himself in the saddle of a steaming pony, yelping excitedly as he fired his pistol at the Indian braves behind him ...

CRACK!

The sound was not in his dream. It was real.

Henry jumped to his feet.

A woman screamed. She was nearby – perhaps just around the corner.

Henry looked across at the saloon. Evidently no one had heard the gunshot or the scream.

"Stand back!" came a rasping voice.

Henry saw a big man charging towards him, brandishing a pistol. In his other hand was a bulging saddlebag.

The man had a dirty neckerchief tied around his face, but Henry was in no doubt this was Dead Eye Dick.

"Stand back!" the man barked.

Crack! The man fired in the air, a warning shot, and Henry stumbled backwards onto the bench.

Dead Eye Dick snatched the loose reins from the hitching rail, and leaped onto his horse, hauling the saddlebag up in front of him.

A phrase flashed into Henry's imaginative brain. A line for his next Western yarn: '*Innocent citizens took cover as the bandit fled on his stallion.*'

"Git!" the bandit cried, slapping the horse's flank. They took off in a flurry of mud, spattering Henry's clothes, and were soon lost among the trees at the end of Hardy Street.

Henry knew the younger bandit, Flash Freddie, would be hard on the heels of his comrade – and here he is now, running as fast as his boots will carry him towards his horse, with a heavy saddlebag over a shoulder, and his face hidden behind that pleasant blue cravat.

Henry is as brave and as quick-witted as any mongoose. He takes hold of the reins of the young man's horse, still loosely looped around the rail, and ties them as tight as he can. Over and under, pull – and again, over and under. Pull tight.

"Watch out!" shouts Flash Freddie. He slams into Henry, sending him sprawling in the mud, and dumps his saddlebag on the ground while he struggles to untangle the reins.

Henry, as agile as the aforementioned mongoose, scrambles to his feet. He grabs the saddlebag, and high-tails it across the street.

The bag is heavy, but Henry is a tough little critter. He is halfway across the street before Flash Freddie with the Pencil Moustache sees him.

CRACK!

A terrifying thought flashes through Henry's brain:
HE IS SHOOTING AT ME!

There is another sharp *crack!* and the bandit's bullet shatters the window of the saloon. Customers dive for cover.

Henry's own father William Appleton appears at the door. Constable Nash joins him, wiping shaving cream from his face. The barber comes out wielding his cut throat razor.

"Father!" Henry gasps, and dumps the saddlebag at his feet.

"Put down the weapon!" bellows the constable.

Henry looks back at Flash Freddie. The young bank robber is standing in the middle of the street, pistol at his side. He is wide eyed and bewildered at how easily he has let some pesky kid take his loot.

He drops his pistol, and six burly Nelson farmers pile on top of him.

"Well done, lads," laughs Constable Nash. "And Henry – what a hero! What a hero!"

William Appleton helps his son to his feet, and our young hero promptly collapses onto a bench, gulping in fresh air, to recover from his first adventure.

Henry grabs the saddlebag, and hightails it
across the street

THREE
THE DEVIL'S DISCIPLE

ON THE VERY SAME DAY OF HENRY'S ENCOUNTER WITH DEAD
Eye Dick and Flash Freddie, and a few days' ride further
south, another villain picked up a pistol with mischief
in mind. He had arrived only weeks ago from Australia,
where he had spent eleven of the past fourteen years in
prison, and for good reason, for he was a thief, a pickpocket, and a violent robber.

"I was a murderer from the first," Richard Burgess
wrote some years later as he awaited the gallows. "A
true disciple of my cruel master Satan." And this
villain's path was soon to cross young Henry Appleton's.

The man was born Richard Hill but now called
himself Burgess. He was a short, powerful man, with
flickering dark eyes, and by no means unattractive to
women. Men too admired him for his bravado, and he

was always in the company of one or two of his own disciples.

His new follower was a fellow Londoner, the Irishman Thomas Kelly, who had spent time in Australian prisons for highway robbery. They quickly became partners in crime.

Keen for easy money, they headed to the Wetherstone gold diggings, inland from Dunedin, and pitched a tent some distance away from the other miners. They spied a local banker who was carrying a large quantity of money, but they missed him when he changed his travel plans.

Then they heard about a man living in a shanty hut nearby, who people said "had plenty of money". His name was William Levisey, and they decided he would be their next target.

Darkness was setting in, and the Wetherstone gully was a flickering sea of candles and lantern lights. Despite the smell of horse manure it was a pretty sight for those who had an eye for beauty, but Burgess and Kelly cared not for such things. They merged into the shadows and waited for their prey.

Before long Levisey stepped out of his hut with a billycan, and set off to fetch water from the creek.

Two figures emerged from the shadows and fell upon the poor digger with the confidence of men well versed in the art of thuggery. One grabbed Levisey's throat to choke him unconscious, while the other dug into the man's trousers looking for cash.

The man struggled for his life, and let out a blood-curdling cry which brought dozens of diggers to the doors of their tents.

"I've been robbed!" Levisey screamed, and there was an uproar of shouts and whistles as men spread out to hunt for the assailants.

Burgess and Kelly were quick to scuttle away into the darkness like rats, running through the trees and skirting around the campsite before returning to their tent. They wriggled inside and lay down to feign sleep.

"That was a right mess," muttered Burgess.

"He had the strength of a tiger," said Kelly.

"No man can get free of a proper grip," Burgess shot back. "And I have a policy, born of long experience: never let a man go free after you have robbed him, for he will come back later to identify you."

"He didn't have time to lay eyes on his visitors," said Kelly.

"That is a blessing. But I stand by my credo: *'dead men tell no tales'.*"

"Next time you do the choking," said Kelly.

"Indeed I will, and I'll teach you the fine art of burking a man with nary a sound coming from his lips."

Kelly said nothing, but pulled the blankets around him.

"Let's get ourselves some well-deserved rest," said Burgess. "Tomorrow we'll track down that banker and catch him to rights."

FOUR
DESPERADOES ON THE RUN

Events did not unfold as Burgess had hoped, however, for when they awoke next morning they could hear the police further down the gully asking diggers about the attack on Levisey.

"Look sharp, Kelly," said Burgess. The two robbers began to haul on their boots, ready to make a getaway.

Outside, just a short distance away, they heard a digger call out to the police.

"There's some likely men in there," said the man. Burgess peeped out from the tent, and sure enough the man was pointing his way. "Those men look the type to do what you're saying."

Burgess, ever bold, and cocky with it, stepped out from the tent and greeted the police.

"Good morning, good sirs," he said, pulling on his shirt. "And a beautiful day it is, to be sure."

He bent to tie up his boot laces. There could well be some running required shortly. He was confident he was in a strong position, as his tent was on higher ground and there were trees around to offer shelter should there be an exchange of lead.

"Good day to you, too, sir," replied Sergeant Joseph Trimble, cautious.

Burgess whispered to Kelly, who was still inside the tent pulling on his clothes: "Kelly, my pistol!"

"Do you have a companion with you, sir?" asked Trimble.

"Why indeed," said Burgess. "A fine young man – my brother in fact – and we're here to join this excellent community in the noble pursuit of gold."

"Would you ask your companion to step outside the tent, please sir?"

"Can I be so bold as to ask the purpose of your request, sir?"

"Indeed," said Sergeant Trimble. "We are here to arrest you for a highway robbery."

"With due respect sir," said Burgess, reaching into the tent to take hold of his pistol, "with due respect, you have no evidence that we have done anyway wrong."

"We have a number of witnesses," said the policeman, indicating the crowd of diggers who were gathering around him.

"Well sir, I am not inclined to go with you," said Burgess.

"Well then, sir, I will make you come with us."

"Come no closer!" yelled Burgess, and produced his pistol.

Trimble held his ground, while around him men dropped to the ground for cover.

Burgess did not fire his weapon, for he was in no hurry to kill a police officer and hang for it. Instead, he picked up his rucksack and began to run further up the hill to the trees.

"Follow me, Kelly!" he yelled. Kelly had the presence of mind to snatch their spare canvas before hurrying after his mate.

"Stop where you are!" called Trimble, but to no effect. The two East London felons had no intention of quietly handing themselves over to the Law.

Running up the steep hillside was a challenge for the fittest of men, and although Burgess and Kelly were tough as old roosters the sergeant was gaining on them. Suddenly Burgess and Kelly turned around and confronted him. Trimble, who was unarmed, stopped in his tracks: Burgess held a revolver, and Kelly had a revolver in each hand.

"Come no closer, man!" yelled Burgess. "I have spent half me sodden life in prison because of men like you, and I have no wish to return."

"Give yourselves up, you fools. There are men all around who are keen to see you locked away. You're done for!"

"I admire your courage, sir," Burgess shouted back, "but we have the firepower here to blow your brains out."

Trimble did not waste time in argument. He slithered back down the hill and grabbed a pistol from another officer, before resuming the chase. Burgess and Kelly continued to scramble up the hill.

Kelly puffed and panted. "Of all the meanest, vilest, needless..."

"Shut up, Kelly," snapped Burgess, himself gasping for air as the pair reached the top of the hill. Trimble was once again closing in on them.

"Stand!" the sergeant bellowed.

Burgess and Kelly turned and presented their pistols. "Keep back!" cried Kelly.

Crack! Trimble fired a warning shot over the heads of the fugitives. "Give yourselves up!"

"Damnation!" complained Burgess. "Why doesn't he let us be?"

They took cover and assessed the situation. From up

here they had a commanding view. The hills were exceedingly steep, and offered little cover for the pursuing policemen.

"We have the upper hand," said Burgess. "Look, the policeman is on his own. There are diggers all over the hills looking for us, baying for our blood, but they are never gonna reach us in time."

Indeed, there were dozens of miners scouring the hill to find the men who had invaded their camp.

"Let's give 'em Jessie then run," said Burgess.

They leaped up and *crack! crack!* fired in Trimble's direction. *Crack!* They saw him retreat. *Crack!* The policeman wasn't keen to be picked off. Burgess and Kelly scampered away like wild rabbits along the ridge and out of sight.

They were sure none of the miners would have the stomach to pursue a couple of armed desperadoes into the fading light, and they were correct. Not a man followed, and the comrades in crime knew they had successfully escaped. Despite their own clumsy antics and the bravery of the policemen, Burgess and Kelly remained free men.

"We'll put some distance between us before pitching tent," said Burgess, once again the cocky leader. They marched on for another hour across the hills and then, confident they were not being followed, they pitched their spare tent.

"I'm knackered," Kelly groaned. "Of all the rough, unwanted, unwarranted, violent episodes in my life..."

"Shut up, Kelly," Burgess laughed. "Our bones are getting old, and we've done a mighty fine day's work. There's nought to show for it by way of gold or silver, but I reckon we've earned a good night's slumber."

They washed down some cheese and bread with the last of their whiskey, and quickly fell asleep.

At dawn they were still sleeping like babies when Sergeant Trimble and Sergeant Major Hugh Bracken crept up on their tent. Bracken slashed open the canvas and pointed two pistols at the escapees, thus ending yet another chapter in the sordid lives of Richard Burgess and Thomas Kelly.

Their beds for the next three years would be in Dunedin Prison.

FIVE
HENRY'S REWARD

On March the 10th, 1862, the determination shown by lawmen Trimble and Bracken in tracking down and capturing Burgess and Kelly made the *Otago Daily Times*.

Meanwhile, further north, in Nelson, young Henry Appleton was also being praised for his part in fighting crime.

"It's a fine thing you did, Henry," said Constable Nash, slapping the boy on the back. "A mighty fine thing."

"Foolhardy, though," said his father William, with a twinkle in his eye.

Young Henry, now safely in the family cottage, could see his father was proud of his actions outside the hairdressing saloon the day before. His mother was too – even though she had scolded him for risking his life to retrieve a bag of cash and gold taken from the bank.

"It's only money," she told him. "You could have been killed."

"The bank owes you a debt of gratitude, Henry," continued Constable Nash. "Not only did you recover their money, but we have been able to track down the other robber. He'd only got a few miles away before we caught him."

Henry was happy to take the credit for this. His detailed description of Dead Eye Dick enabled the police to identify the culprit beyond doubt.

"We'd like to thank you for your brave act, sonny," came an unfamiliar voice.

There at the door of Bluebell Cottage was the unmistakable form of the bank manager, Mister Lester J. Chadwick, recently transferred from Dunedin to build up the bank's business in Nelson. He brushed the perspiration from his glistening forehead and announced:

"We have a reward."

A reward? Henry's thoughts raced immediately to the one object he longed to own.

"A rifle?"

Henry was embarrassed to realise he had said this

out loud, and blushed as the adults around him laughed. Or, in the case of his mother, tut-tutted.

"No no, not a gun," said the bank manager. "We could never give a gun to – to a boy."

"I am not a boy, sir," Henry protested. Indeed, even at his tender age he was already mending fences and doing other chores around the farm.

Mister Chadwick chuckled and patted Henry's head.

"I'm sure you'll have your own firearm when you're old enough, sonny. But in the meantime – " He stepped back to give Henry a clear view of the front yard.

And thus Henry first laid eyes on the creature that was to become his friend and helpmate in his adventures of the next few years. A strapping pony, snorting and stomping, and ready to be ridden by a young cowboy.

"Duke!" cried Henry. A horse was not as exciting as a gun, certainly, but every adventurer needed a horse, and now Henry had his own. He already had a name chosen. A name that featured in the stories of the Wild West that raced around in his head.

"Duke!" The pony cocked his head. Henry gave a loud, shrill whistle through his front teeth – just like the cowboys did in his dime novels. Duke paid no attention, but Henry was not troubled.

"I'll teach him to come when I whistle," he told his parents, and ran to embrace the horse.

* * *

"Why did you do it, sonny?"

"I'm nearly 11 years old, sir," Henry responded.

The newspaperman grinned, made a note in his book, and repeated his question.

"What made you risk your life by confronting an armed man?"

Henry thought it over.

"I like reading adventure stories, sir. About cowboys. The Wild West."

The reporter scribbled. He could see this would make a good angle, and he stoked the fire.

"Would you like to be a cowboy one day, sonny?"

Henry looked out the window at Duke, grazing peacefully in the front yard.

"Yessir," he said. "I already have my own horse."

The reporter couldn't help laughing out loud. "That's a grand start," he said.

"I'm teaching him to come when I whistle," said Henry. He gave a shrill whistle through his front teeth. The horse merely gazed at him quizzically before continuing to nibble at the grass.

"Give him time," said the reporter.

QUICK THINKING BY PLUCKY 'COWBOY'
RESULTS IN ARREST OF ARMED ROBBERS

The *Nelson Examiner* ran the story in the next edition, and Henry and his family were famous in the district.

Henry folded the newspaper article and tucked it away between the pages of his dime novel, *Gunfight on the High Plateau* by the famed American author Johnny Slick. He sensed he was destined for a life of adventure, although the last line of the newspaper item embarrassed Henry a little. It read:

"Master Appleton is teaching his horse to come when he whistles."

Henry knew he had work to do.

SIX
BAD NEWS

WHILE BURGESS AND KELLY LANGUISHED IN JAIL, THE NEXT three and a half years for Henry were quite unremarkable. He went to school, did his chores, read dime novels, dreamed of life as a Wild West adventurer, secured a part time job at the local bank, and taught Duke a few tricks.

He was no closer to owning a rifle, but with his 14th birthday approaching he began to build his hopes that this might be the milestone: the day his parents presented him with a gun. Perhaps not an Enfield Cavalry carbine like his father's, but—

"It's your birthday tomorrow," said William Appleton. "I'm going to teach you to handle a rifle."

Henry's heart leapt. He saw an expression of deep sadness cross his mother's face, but thought nothing of it. Even as he and his father boarded the trap, and Victoria Appleton dabbed her eyes and waved goodbye, he could think of nothing but rifles. His father was about to introduce him to a real weapon, and with his birthday coming the next day...

They trotted across the fields. Henry was proud that it was his own horse Duke in the harness. They had sold their old horse Solomon to cover the cost of a bank loan, and Duke was now strong enough for any task.

"Hup, Duke!" called Henry joyfully as he flicked the reins.

His father sat next to him silently, his precious rifle at his side. Finally he called a halt, and the two of them got down from the cart and made their way to a piece of open ground. But instead of reaching for his rifle, the older man put an arm on Henry's shoulder and cleared his throat.

"Son, I have some bad news."

Henry gulped. The prospect of receiving a rifle as a gift tomorrow grew dim. He waited while his father took a deep breath.

"I know you have been hoping for your own rifle, son, and I would dearly like to buy one for you. But it cannot happen yet. I regret that we do not have the means."

Henry stifled a sniff, and looked at the ground. He

knew his parents were struggling to pay their bills. He had been unrealistic to expect that they would be able to afford a gun for their son.

"I understand," he said. But he could not stop his eyes welling up.

His father embraced him. This did not happen very often, and Henry buried his tear-stained face in his father's jacket.

He resolved that he would continue to save money from his small job at the bank. One day, perhaps, he would be able to buy a gun himself.

"I have worse news," he heard his father say through the folds of his jacket.

What could possibly be worse than the news that he would not receive a gun as a birthday present? Henry stood back and searched his father's face for clues.

William Appleton straightened himself, and summoned up a reassuring smile.

"It'll be fine," he said. "Just fine."

Henry waited. He knew it would not be fine, whatever it was.

"I'm going away," said his father.

Henry froze.

"I'm going to work on the goldfields."

Henry's mouth opened but no words came.

And the very next day, after wishing his son a happy

fourteenth birthday, William Appleton picked up his rucksack, kissed his wife goodbye, tousled his son's hair, and trudged off down the track towards the goldfields.

Henry and his mother watched him in disbelief. When he was lost from view, Victoria turned on her heels without a word and strode into the garden to resume digging with angry energy.

They received several letters from William Appleton as he struggled in the goldfields, but they never saw him alive again.

SEVEN
A PLAN TAKES SHAPE

HENRY'S MOTHER HAD BAKED A LOAF, AND SHE BROUGHT OUT his favourite cheese for a midday meal to celebrate his birthday. But neither of them was tempted by the aromas wafting through the cottage. Even when she presented him with her gift, a hand-sewn shirt with a delicately-trimmed collar, he could produce only the smallest smile.

"It's for the best," she began. "Your father has been deeply troubled of late due to our impecunious situation. This is his way of showing us he cares, and he's determined to provide for us."

"But you've always told me the goldfields are no place for an educated man."

"I know, I know," his mother cried. "But your father could think of no other option."

Henry got up from the table and marched into his room, threw himself on the bed and sobbed. His mother buried her head in her work-worn hands.

After some time Henry fell into a deep sleep, and his mother went back into the garden. She lacked the will to dig with her usual ferocity, and after a few half-hearted blows she leant on the spade and cried.

The sun had sunk behind the hills when Henry woke to the sound of his mother moving around in the kitchen. The smell of fresh bread still hung in the air, and Henry shuffled back to the table to eat.

"Thank you for my gift," he said. "It's an excellent shirt and I shall treasure it always."

"Happy birthday, son," said his mother as she kissed his forehead. She was pleased to see he had woken in a more cheerful disposition, and hoped this meant he was determined to face his father's absence in a positive manner.

However no such resolve was present in Henry's mind. Instead, a new plan had taken shape as he emerged from his sleep. He would follow his father to the goldfields, and if he could not persuade him to return to their cottage he would stay there and help his father in the diggings. Furthermore, he would leave the very next morning.

"It's for the best, I know," he assured his mother,

feeling guilty about deceiving her, but trembling with excitement about his desperate plan.

That evening, as his mother disappeared into the garden to check the animals, Henry closed his bedroom door and began preparing for an early departure. He put aside the shirt his mother had sewn for him, and the hat which his father had bought from the thrift store. It would probably be a hot day, and he had a long way to travel.

EIGHT
OFF TO THE GOLDFIELDS

VICTORIA APPLETON WOKE AS SHE ALWAYS DID TO THE SOUND of the rooster crowing in the garden. She dressed and lit a fire in the oven, and spent an hour digging and watering the vegetables before collecting two fresh eggs and returning to the cottage to prepare breakfast.

"Henry, time to get up!" she called. She allowed another few minutes before calling again, and finally opened his bedroom door to rouse him. To her dismay the bed was empty. A piece of paper lay where she was sure to see it. Her hands shook as she read it.

"Dear Mother," Henry wrote. "I am going to the goldfields to find father and bring him home."

That was all. He could have written more, to explain his emotions and lay out his plans in more detail, but the brief note was the work of a young man of action.

Already Henry was miles away, spurring Duke to reach the goldfields in quick time.

He had been tempted to take his father's rifle with him, but reasoned that if his father had deemed it best to leave the rifle at home then he would follow suit.

It was not long before he began to regret that decision, as he encountered several travellers along the way who were not only of dubious character but were carrying weapons.

The track was narrow, and Henry slowed Duke to a walk as he passed one such traveller, a small man with a shapeless hat and oversized jacket. He was on foot, and wheezing from exertion.

"What gives, sonny?" he demanded as Henry passed him, taking care that his stallion did not nudge the man off the track and into the bushes. "What gives?"

His mother had taught Henry that "honesty is the best policy," so he tipped his hat and responded, "I am going to the goldfields."

"All on your lonesome?" wheezed the man with the floppy hat.

Henry did not like his question, much less the tone in which it was asked, so he replied "Yes, sir," and kicked his horse into a trot. As he reached the next bend he looked back and saw the man in the floppy hat squatting on a rock to rest.

"Good riddance," he said to himself, and continued on his way.

He drew himself taller in the saddle and counted his blessings. He was a healthy young man, riding a spirited horse on a brand new adventure. His fingers played with the neatly-sewn hems on the collar of his new shirt, and he tried not to dwell on his mother's anxiety when she found him gone.

"She will understand," he told himself.

A Western story came to mind, one modestly titled *Lone Rider*, and Henry allowed himself to compare the lone rider's mission to his own. The young hero of this story was a similar age, one of a group of fearless young horsemen who operated the Pony Express, carrying mail and newspapers between Missouri and California. Henry had been told the Pony Express lasted less than two years, but it was the stuff of legends. Henry was certain that, had he been born in the United States, he would have been one of those Pony Express riders.

Quite suddenly Henry became aware that he was exhausted, after a sleepless night and a morning's hard riding, and so was Duke. He led his horse off the track and found a secluded spot behind the rocks to lie down. He placed his hat over his eyes and was soon dreaming again, this time whipping his pony across the prairies.

He was working for the Pony Express, carrying a

saddlebag full of important mail, but his horse was beginning to tire as they galloped at speed towards the next relief station where he would switch mounts.

Another horse drew alongside him, and a gruff voice broke through his thoughts.

"Sleeping like a baby," it said.

Henry was awake in an instant, and whipped his hat from his eyes.

Standing above him as he sprawled in the grass was the wheezy man in the floppy hat. It was not he who had spoken, though. There was another visitor, a large man with a bushy beard.

"Like a baby," the man said again, and his belly trembled with laughter.

Henry sat up for a better look, and immediately wished he was back at Bluebell Cottage eating his favourite bread and cheese.

The second figure was a man known to him from his adventure outside the hairdressing saloon some four years ago. A man Henry had helped bring to justice: an armed robber who should surely still be in jail. A man notable for the fact that his left eye was a steely blue, and his right eye was dead.

A villain Henry would always remember as Dead Eye Dick.

NINE
HENRY LOSES HIS HORSE

"Well, well, well," said Dead Eye Dick, and spat a wad of chewed tobacco in the dirt. "So we're off to the gold-fields, are we?"

"On our lonesome," added Floppy Hat.

"On our lonesome?" Dead Eye Dick feigned surprise.

At this point Henry let out his breath. It was clear that Dead Eye Dick did not recognize him as the young upstart who had foiled his escape after the bank robbery, and later identified him in court. Henry had grown a good handspan taller since then, and bore little resemblance to that nervous boy in the courtroom.

"Yes," he said. "I'm joining my father." Perhaps that would make these men think twice before they carried out any unpleasantness.

"We're off to see daddy," mocked Floppy Hat.

"And we have a fine horse that daddy bought us," said Dead Eye Dick, scratching Duke's jaw.

If only you knew that Duke was my reward for putting you in prison, said Henry to himself.

"A fine horse," repeated Dead Eye Dick, and without a further word he hauled his bulky frame into Duke's saddle. "We'll borrow him a while."

He turned Duke back towards the path, and Henry leapt to his feet.

"No!" he cried.

Floppy Hat gave Henry such a shove that he stumbled backwards and fell against the rocks, causing him to gasp.

"Stay there, sonny," Floppy Hat ordered.

Henry sat up, ready to get to his feet.

"You can't take my horse!" he said.

"Yes we can, squirt," replied Floppy Hat, and pointed his pistol at Henry's hat lying in the grass.

Crack! The pistol spat flame, and Henry's hat jumped in the air.

"If you wanna die where you are, you'll do that again," said the rogue. He glared at Henry for a long moment, and then hurried after Dead Eye Dick.

Henry's whole body was shaking with the shock of being fired at in such a random manner. But despite his misery, he could not help but be amused as he watched

Floppy Hat attempt to climb onto Duke's back. Receiving no encouragement or help from his companion or Duke, Floppy Hat resigned himself to running alongside the horse, holding on to the saddle.

In one last bid to change his fortune, Henry whistled as loud as he was able; his special cowboy whistle. He saw Duke's ears twitch as he recognized the call, but the horse continued trotting happily along with his new masters.

Duke and the two horse thieves disappeared around the corner. Henry picked up his hat and examined the holes where Floppy Hat's bullet had passed through, then slumped against the rock to consider his situation, which he perceived to be as grim and hopeless as it could be.

He had no horse, and no plan. He did not even have the energy to cry.

TEN
THE CAVALRY ARRIVES

"Henry? Henry Appleton!"

Henry had resolved to run all the way to the gold-fields, hoping to catch up with Dead Eye Dick and then – well, Henry's plan went no further than this. As he pushed himself to exhaustion along the hot and dusty track, he was in part yelling at himself for getting into such a pickle, and cursing his horse Duke for abandoning him so readily. He was aggrieved that Fate could deal him such an unlucky blow, but he did not dare to even think about Dead Eye Dick and his evil intent.

"Henry?"

He halted when he heard a familiar voice behind him.

"What the devil are you doing here, young man?" asked Constable Nash.

Henry blinked. Fate had brought Dead Eye Dick into his life again, but now that same fickle entity had dished up a welcome surprise in the person of Constable Nash.

In Henry's Western stories, this was the moment the Cavalry arrived with bugle blaring, to rescue whoever needed rescuing.

"Constable Nash, sir!" Henry cried out.

Even more wonderfully, Nash had in his company two soldiers and four shopkeepers from Nelson township, two of them armed.

"We're in pursuit of an escaped prisoner," the policeman explained.

In a heartbeat, Henry knew the name of prisoner they sought, and marvelled at the way his path had collided so providentially with the cavalry.

"Hop up, son," said Constable Nash.

Henry pulled on his hat, grateful that no one mentioned its newly acquired ventilation, and clambered up behind Constable Nash. As they rode along the path he told them about his latest encounter with Dead Eye Dick.

He knew everything was going to turn out well, and he was sure his mother would understand.

He clung to Constable Nash's stiff blue jacket as they trotted into the miners' camp, reassured by the clanking of the policeman's cutlass as it slapped against the flank of his horse. But when the constable drew out his pistol he was more afraid than excited.

"He's armed and desperate," said Nash. He called a halt to his posse, and helped Henry to the ground. "Remain here with Hans."

A tall German miner stepped forward and put a huge hand on Henry's shoulder. He said nothing, but his reassuring growl gave Henry all the comfort he needed.

Nash and his party trotted away in single file, eyes keenly studying the tents and checking the occasional miner who was too drunk or exhausted to be down at the river with his pan searching for gold.

Henry stayed close to his big German protector, and looked around. So this was it, the miners' camp about which he had heard so much. Alarming tales of drunken brawls, fistfights, knives and pistols ... robberies, violent arguments over claims ... and even the occasional murder. But right now, in the lazy warmth of the afternoon, it was more peaceful than a church meeting.

Some of the miners who crouched at the door of their tents reading, or dozing on their folded jackets, seemed as young as Henry. One or two men were older, bearded and ragged, with an air of sadness and desperation.

Hans grunted again, and shepherded Henry away

from the central track which ran the length of the encampment. He offered Henry a pewter mug and sloshed some water into it from a dented can. Henry grabbed it and gulped it down.

"Thank you," he said. "I'm looking for my father."

Hans looked blank.

"Papa."

There was a sudden commotion. Men yelling. The thundering of a horse's hooves.

Henry and Hans looked up, and saw a large man on a powerful horse charging along the row of tents towards them.

Henry gasped, for the stallion on which Dead Eye Dick was making his escape was none other than Henry's own faithless steed.

Duke, in full flight, carrying an escaped felon!

Henry jumped to his feet, and without thinking he let loose with his special cowboy whistle.

What happened next would lead Henry to forgive Duke's every perceived shortcoming. For the horse, upon hearing his young master's whistle, immediately stopped in his tracks, his muscular haunches heaving.

The bank robber, riding confidently with only a light hand on the reins, was launched into the air and sailed over the horse's head.

Henry watched with a mixture of glee and awe as

the big man flew above him like a gigantic wood pigeon, a large bundle of flapping coat and flailing limbs, his belt and buckles twitching and flicking as they followed closely behind.

It seemed as though the pigeon would remain airborne forever, but Dead Eye Dick crashed to the hard earth with a bone-crunching thump. It knocked the wind from him. He lay gasping for air, finding it even more difficult to breathe when Hans the German miner sat on him.

Henry whooped for joy and embraced his beloved horse. Constable Nash and his posse were soon on the scene to restrain the recaptured bank robber.

Within the hour they were on the track again, heading back to Nelson and towing Dead Eye Dick behind them, securely tied up in a borrowed wagon.

Henry was with them. He had pleaded for time to find his father, but Constable Nash would not hear of it.

"Your mother will be despairing," he said.

He was right, for Victoria Appleton was in tears when they finally reached Bluebell Cottage and Constable Nash handed over her bruised and bedraggled son.

There was much rejoicing in the cottage that night. But Henry had not found his father, and his mother made him swear never to attempt such a mission again.

Henry watched with a mixture of glee and
awe as Dead Eye Dick flew like a gigantic
wood pigeon

ELEVEN
LEARN TO DO GOOD

HENRY WAS TRUE TO HIS WORD, AND DID NOT MAKE ANOTHER bid to reach the goldfields. Then, only a few months later, came the news that his father was dead. Henry could not help wondering, *If I had been able to reach him, perhaps I could have persuaded him to come home?*

He was left with this lingering question. He would often pause at the cemetery on his way into town, lay a small bunch of wild flowers by the burial spot of his adoptive father, and ask aloud:

"Would you have come home, Father?"

William Appleton was not his birth father, but he was the only father Henry had ever known, and he had played a big role in his life.

This was, after all, the man who had brought him all the way from Old England to an exciting new life in a beautiful country. The man who had inspired him with stories of bravery and love, the man who had passed on to him a passion for justice.

Henry stood in front of the Celtic cross and re-read the familiar lines. *'Here lies William Henry Appleton, b 1819 d 1865. A good man in the eyes of the Lord.'*

On the grave was a passage from The Book of Isaiah, which William Appleton had often read to Henry: *'Learn to do good; correct oppression; bring justice to the fatherless.'*

Correct oppression. Henry had always been taken by this phrase, and decided this would be his guiding philosophy. But as he soon discovered, it was a philosophy that could bring a heap of trouble, and usually involved a degree of pain.

It was one morning in April, as the date of Henry's fifteenth birthday approached, and he was spending a good deal of time musing on life and its purpose, that Henry's guiding philosophy was put to the test.

He was seated in the school room, surrounded by chattering classmates, waiting for the return of their teacher Miss Darby. He had no close friends here; the hours before and after school were mostly spent helping his mother on the farm, and there were few opportunities to get to know others his own age.

Rachel Simpson was pretty, he noted, but her main interest seemed to be gossiping with her friends. He had tried to strike up a conversation once, but it became apparent very quickly that she was not the least bit interested in horses, American cowboys or guns.

"Perkins!"

A harsh cry interrupted Henry's thoughts. He looked over to see Jasper Thornton waving a large, very ripe grapefruit in the air. On the other side of the room, young Perkins – no one knew his Christian name – stared fixedly at his school books while Thornton repeated his cry:

"Perkins, you sick chicken!"

Some of the other boys sniggered. They all knew Perkins was missing some capacity in his mind, and they were keen not to cross his tormentor Jasper Thornton, who was older and more sturdily built than any of them.

Henry gulped as two words whispered in his inner ear:

Correct oppression.

Well, he reasoned, this wasn't exactly a case of oppression of global significance. Then—

The over-ripe grapefruit sailed through the air, above the heads of the other students, and *slop!* smashed into the side of Perkins' head. The poor boy cried out in dismay as the juice and pulp of the missile slithered down his face and onto his shirt. Half the class laughed out loud, the other half gasped in disbelief and sympathy.

Correct oppression!

Henry Appleton jumped to his feet and yelled at Thornton:

"Stop it, you bully!"

Henry sat up to see a circle of wide-eyed
faces staring down at him

The laughing stopped. All eyes turned to Thornton for his response. For a moment he was frozen; then he hurled himself at Henry, sending desks and chairs flying. One large fist landed squarely on Henry's jaw and sent him sprawling among the chair legs.

Henry blinked as stars danced before his eyes, and his hands clawed at the legs of a nearby desk. He must stand, and continue his fight to correct oppression.

"Master Thornton, take your seat *immediately*!"

Miss Darby was back, and Henry knew there would be no more pain. He rubbed his jaw and sat up to see a circle of wide-eyed faces staring down at him: Perkins, an expression of gratitude on his fruit-spattered face; and Rachel Simpson, taking a close interest in this boy who loved horses and guns.

"Father would be proud of you," his mother told him that evening as she tended to the cut on his swollen jaw.

Henry gave a small smile. He might be fatherless, but on this day he believed he had truly taken one small step to correct oppression. And he was determined to make something of his life. Perhaps as an explorer. Perhaps as a lawman.

Henry still enjoyed reading the stories of his Western heroes, and imagined himself riding across the plains of America. All he needed to become an adventurer, he reckoned, was a rifle. It still rankled with him that although he was now the man of the house and carried out many of the chores around the farm, his mother forbade him from having his father's rifle.

He had of course, like many a restless young man before him, ignored his mother's admonitions. Whenever he could, he would take the rifle from its secure hiding place and spend happy hours polishing it and admiring its design.

It was an new model Enfield cavalry carbine, much faster to load than the old muzzle-loading weapons. William Appleton had arranged for the weapon to be sent from England, and Henry remembered his father's excitement as he opened the box containing the rifle. Victoria Appleton was upset about this extravagant purchase, especially as they had only recently been forced to sell their old horse Solomon to keep up with their payments on the cottage.

But William Appleton responded:

"A man needs a gun."

Henry never forgot that, and would oft times remind his mother:

"A man needs a gun."

His horse Duke was now a full-grown stallion, and Henry's pride and joy. Once Henry had a rifle, his life as an adventurer could begin.

So Henry whispered "thank you, father" as he laid the flowers by the grave.

He was not to know how soon his courage and sense of justice would be tested again.

For Richard Burgess had been released from prison in Dunedin and was now aboard the *Wallabi* and headed for the Nelson district. He had with him Thomas Kelly, his old mate, and a new accomplice by the name of Joseph Sullivan. This man was also a Londoner, transported to Australia for robbing a shop, and although he lacked the devilish charm of Burgess he was in his own way very persuasive.

Both men could lie and cheat their way out of most situations, and both men were ruthless, as their exploits in New Zealand would soon prove.

Kelly, Burgess and Sullivan aboard the
Wallabi, bound for Nelson

TWELVE
AMERICAN DREAMS

Henry's fifteenth birthday came and went. He had hoped, in a forlorn kind of way, that his mother might give him his father's rifle. Or even his father's boots. But it was not to be: his mother was still guarding those treasures.

She presented him instead with a handsome hat, bought from Everett Brothers' new shop in Bridge Street, and Henry was quietly convinced that he looked very manly in it. He would never say as much, lest his mother remind him 'Pride comes before a fall', but he took to wearing his new hat day and night.

At 15 Henry was already very much 'a man' in the eyes of the town. Big and strong enough to dig the garden, mend the fences, ride the horse. But ownership of a gun eluded him. He was certain that his father would have allowed him to use his rifle, but his father was dead and his mother was of a different view. "A gun does not make you a man," she would say whenever he raised the subject.

His mother worked ceaselessly in the garden, and Henry often laboured alongside her. But whenever he could find an excuse to go inside he would retrieve his father's rifle from under his mother's bed. Even a few minutes handling the weapon and firing imaginary bullets out his window at imaginary attackers was enough to keep up his spirits.

Henry slumped onto his bed. He heard his mother put water in a pot on the hearth, and from under his mattress he pulled a dime novel.

On the cover was a sketch of an American trapper with shoulder-length hair and drooping moustache, dressed in animal furs. He posed, heroic, with a long rifle. The heading proclaimed *Wild Bill Hickok and Shootout at Dead Man's Creek*.

This was one of many adventure stories written by Johnny Slick, and a favourite. Slick knew how to write action stories, and in a way that touched the hearts of young men like Henry.

Slick's stories were particularly appealing to Henry because their heroes were rugged men who were tough and resourceful. As hardy as bears. They were men who survived blizzards and baking sun, and told tall stories around the campfire at night.

They travelled light and carried nothing more than a sleeping blanket and a water bottle.

And a gun, of course.

"A man needs a gun," Henry reminded himself.

THIRTEEN
ANOTHER STRANGER ARRIVES

JUST AS HENRY WOULD NEVER FORGET THE DAY THE MINERS brought home his father's body, there was another day that also would be etched on his memory forever. It was the day the physician arrived.

Henry had been deep in conversation with his mother when, through the front door, he saw movement out in the woods beyond their front fence.

"Mother – look!"

In the shadow of the trees, maybe fifty yards away, was a man on horseback.

"Henry – be careful!"

His mother was not usually anxious about strangers; they passed this way all the time, and often stopped and rented a bed in the barn. Had his mother seen the rifle at the man's side? This was nothing unusual either; many travellers carried some sort of weapon. Perhaps she had a premonition. Perhaps she knew this man would change the course of Henry's life.

Perhaps Henry knew it too.

Zephaniah Smith, for that was his name, cut a dashing figure. He sat straight-backed in the saddle, like a cavalry officer, and his rifle rested in a leather holster on the horse's flank.

Hanging from his saddle was an old leather doctor's bag.

This was June the 6th, in the year of our Lord 1866. It was only a year since the assassination of Abraham Lincoln. Joseph Lister would soon begin promoting the use of antiseptics to prevent the spread of infections. And Alfred Nobel would invent dynamite.

These were momentous events. But none of them concerned Zephaniah Smith. He was in New Zealand, on the far side of the world, on a mission of his own; and young Henry Appleton was about to become deeply involved.

Dr Smith nudged his horse and trotted towards the cottage.

On another horse behind him, leading a packhorse, was a slim young Māori man, around the same age as Henry. His face was largely hidden under a wide-brimmed straw hat; the sort Henry had seen the local Chinese workers wearing.

Henry and his mother stepped outside to greet the travellers.

Smith tipped his hat and dismounted smoothly.

"Morning, Ma'am." His clipped voice was that of an English gentleman.

Henry sidled closer to study the visitor's rifle. He recognized it as an Enfield cavalry carbine similar to his father's. The visitor bowed.

"Allow me to introduce myself. The name is Smith. Doctor Smith."

Henry knew the visitor's refined manners would impress his mother, and he watched her brush the dirt from her hands. Her initial caution had disappeared.

"And this..." Smith turned to his young companion, who was examining the packhorse's hoof. "This is Rama, my guide. And translator."

Rama nodded, but before Henry could take a closer look he moved out of sight, behind the packhorse.

Henry's mother curtsied. He hadn't seen her do that for many a day.

"Victoria Appleton. Pleased to make your acquaintance."

"Delighted," the doctor replied, snapping the heels of his boots together and offering her another bow.

"And my son, Henry."

Smith nodded in Henry's direction, and quickly got down to business.

"We have travelled quite a distance. Might we water our horses?"

"Certainly," Henry's mother answered. "Henry?"

Henry did not answer immediately. He was puzzling over the *Z. Smith* which was engraved on the doctor's bag. Was this man really a doctor? And what did the *Z* stand for?

"Henry, water please?" repeated his mother.

Henry went off to fetch water.

Smith indicated the packhorse.

"She needs rest."

Henry's mother was keen for conversation. Very few travellers as well-educated as Doctor Smith passed this way.

"You are from London?"

"Indeed," he replied with yet another small bow. "More recently Australia."

Henry returned and gave Rama a bucket of water.

"Kia ora," the young man replied, then led the packhorse to the door of the barn, and tied it up.

Smith indicated Duke.

"Perhaps your boy could transport our bags into town?"

Henry bridled, for he was confident that his brave exploits and his hard work on the farm had surely entitled him to be referred to as 'a young man', not a boy.

Nevertheless, he prepared Duke for the journey to town while his mother and Dr Smith continued to chat.

"I see you call this Bluebell Cottage," said Smith. "I miss the bluebells in spring."

Henry's mother nodded.

"I brought acorns from the Home Country, and they are doing well." She pointed at a sturdy young oak tree, perhaps as tall as a man, growing in the yard. "But most flowers from home cannot grow here. The climate is too harsh."

She missed London's busy streets, the parks, the grand manors and quaint city apartments. The magnificent concerts and elegant soirees. And of course the flowers that grew so easily in England but struggled to cope with the New Zealand climate.

Smith and Rama climbed back on their horses.

"Let's away, Henry," said the doctor quietly.

With some difficulty Henry mounted Duke, squeezing in front of the visitors' bags, and led the way to the farm gate.

In the garden, his mother watched them move away, then resumed digging with angry energy.

FOURTEEN
SACRED MOUNTAIN

"I AM A SCOUT," THOUGHT HENRY AS THEY TRAVELLED. "A scout, with the eyes of a hawk." The scouts were among his favourite characters in *Gunfight on the High Plateau* and other dime novels he had read. They were lone riders who would gallop ahead of the wagon train to make sure the path ahead was safe. They were rugged, independent men who risked their lives every day. Men of few words who had to be observant, vigilant ... and handy with the rifle.

Henry sucked in his breath as he tapped his saddle and imagined the high powered rifle that nestled there.

Henry recalled the stories he had read about the Indian scouts who led the wagon trains West through hostile territory, bound for Oregon or California. The main dangers they faced were dust storms, high rivers and lack of water or food – but they were still mindful of the Indians whose lands they were traversing. It paid to be vigilant.

Henry tilted his hat, narrowed his eyes, and scanned the rocks and trees on the horizon. Danger could come from any direction.

"An ideal spot for an ambush," said Dr Smith.

"An ideal spot for an ambush," said Dr
Smith

"Huh?" Henry realised they had stopped next to a giant volcanic rock which protruded from the earth beside the path. It was an impressive rock – bigger than a stage coach, Henry thought – and not remarkable in any other way. But Dr Smith was right: it would give excellent cover to a highwayman. Henry the Scout looked around with fresh eyes. The track was narrow, with room for only a cart or a pair of horses to pass. This was, undoubtedly, a suitable location for a holdup.

Henry was impressed that Dr Smith would think of such things in the middle of a relaxed outing on a sunny day, when the most immediate dangers were the deep wagon tracks in the ground. He began to respect Dr Smith even more. He was clearly a military man, always contemplating strategy and tactics. Where he would place his soldiers. Where the horses. Where the cannons.

Henry, besides reading cowboy adventure stories, had also read accounts of the battles in New Zealand. There had been terrible encounters between Māori warriors and white soldiers. At Ohaeawai, Ruapekapeka Pa, Gate Pa.

The British soldiers had been slow to learn it was unwise to employ the battle tactics of Europe, where rows of working class boys in red jackets would stand like lambs in the middle of a field, to be mown down by bullets and bayonets. You had to use different tactics in the dense bush and rugged hills of New Zealand. The soldiers' foes were Māori warriors who would launch a surprise attack and then melt back into the forest.

Henry led Smith and Rama through the dark forest. Past Pritchard's Cottage, an abandoned building which was soon to feature large in Henry's heroic adventures, and into open country, dotted with cottages and small farms.

There was a funeral in progress on the nearby ceme-tery knoll, and Henry paused to converse with his friend, police officer John Nash. Nash had a big heart and he was a straight-shooter. Henry had liked this man ever since the episode outside West's Hair Dressing Saloon, and later his rescue on the track to the goldfields.

A sergeant now, Nash sat on horseback, apart from the mourners. Straight-backed, vigilant, wearing the military cap and blue jacket of the Nelson Provincial Armed Constabulary.

"Morning, Sergeant, sir."

Henry introduced Dr Smith to the sergeant, then dismounted and walked with his mother's wildflowers to the Celtic headstone nearby, where his father's body lay. William Appleton, the man who had adopted him, brought him to New Zealand – was that courageous, or reckless? – and then gone to the goldfields and never returned.

He read the familiar words: *'Here lies William Henry Appleton. A good man in the eyes of the Lord.'*

Henry bit his lip as he contemplated his father's advice from beyond the grave: *'Learn to do good; correct oppression; bring justice to the fatherless.'*

"The fatherless"? he thought. *That's me.* And bringing justice? Well, so far that had only gotten Henry into a whole lot of trouble. He touched his jaw. Sometimes it ached where Jasper Thornton had punched him that memorable day in the classroom.

FIFTEEN
THE BEST IN TOWN

THE THREE HORSEMEN GALLOPED ACROSS THE OPEN countryside, their steeds steaming with exertion, leaving clumps of flying turf in their wake. Doctor Smith, Rama and Henry. What a romantic scene, Henry thought to himself as he gripped the reins and admired the rippling muscles on Duke's neck. Someone should paint this picture for the cover of a dime novel like *Gunfight on the High Plateau*. Or better still, *Henry Appleton, Soldier of the Prairie*.

He laughed out loud, then snapped out of his day dream. He must remain focused on the task at hand – to escort two travellers to the safety of Nelson Township. And this he did, unworried today by any scalp-hunting Indians or gold-grabbing outlaws.

They slowed to a trot as they entered town, and

shortly drew level with a sun-faded hoarding: *The Bank of Nelson. Since 1842.* This was where Henry worked, part-time. He was grateful for the employment, but disliked the people he worked with.

There was the surly guard, Dodge, slouched on the veranda, picking at his finger nails with a pocketknife. Where ever did they find him, Henry wondered. He was sure the man must have a shady past, and most certainly had spent time in prison.

Henry spied the manager, Mr Lester J. Chadwick in his office, staring out at the people of Nelson who needed his money. Chadwick, the man who had once presented Henry with a pony – his beloved Duke – as a reward for helping to catch a bank robber. The same man who was now planning to auction the Appletons' farm.

Chadwick caught his eye, and looked pointedly at his watch. But when Smith gave him a steely look, Chadwick retreated into the shadows.

At the corner of Trafalgar and Bridge Streets, Henry stopped outside a large two storey wooden building: the Trafalgar Hotel, right next to Everett Bros. The hotel was one of the most impressive buildings in Nelson.

"This is the best in town, sir."

They dismounted, and Smith handed his reins to Rama.

Henry spotted an advertising bill tied to one of the hotel's veranda posts, fluttering in the breeze.

He could see two words which set his heart pounding: *Johnny Slick.* Henry hurried closer to read more:

> *TONIGHT ONLY – hear the remarkable adventures of the United States' most celebrated writer: Mister Johnny Slick.*

"Johnny Slick's in town!" cried Henry. He read on:

> *A storyteller who has rubbed shoulders with the most famous outlaws and lawmen of America's Wild West. Author of numerous adventure yarns, including 'Wild Bill and the Indian outlaw.'*

Henry put aside his worries about the farm, and his curiosity about his new companions. He resolved that, come Hell or high water, he would arrange to meet his literary hero, Johnny Slick.

SIXTEEN
HENRY MEETS HIS IDOL

WHICH BRINGS US, DEAR READER, TO THIS HUMBLE WRITER Johnny Slick's first meeting with the hero of our story. It took place at the Rising Sun Hotel.

I had not been there previously, and undoubtedly there were more reputable establishments in which to spend my three nights in Nelson. But as a storyteller I enjoyed the company of ordinary working men; adventurers and braggarts whose stories over a jug of ale would often find their way into my books. They would tell me their experiences in the goldfields of Australia, California and New Zealand: the brawls, the comradeship, the untimely deaths of recently-rich diggers, the seedy schemes of less scrupulous diggers, the ambushes and beatings, and the encounters with unfortunate young widows who became bar girls in order to survive.

Many of these characters would one day populate my novels for the entertainment of my fellow Americans.

Thus it was, after a day of socialising, I retired to my room to partake of a glass of whiskey while preparing for that night's lecture. I knew the hall would be packed – mostly with young men, eager to hear my elaborate and admittedly embellished stories from the American West.

The advertising bills, posted all around town, would ensure a full house. *'TONIGHT ONLY!'* the posters shouted, describing me as *'the United States' most celebrated writer.'* Perhaps that was a step too far, but who would challenge me? The rest was true: *'A storyteller who has rubbed shoulders with the most famous outlaws and lawmen of America's Wild West.'*

By this time of course the Wild West of cowboys and Indians had largely gone, but the romance of that era endured. The exploits of men like William F. Cody, later known as Buffalo Bill, would sell a million books and fill a thousand halls.

My own encounter with Wild Bill Hickok, while less eventful than Buffalo Bill's many exploits, could still raise a cheer and a laugh from my audiences. It suited me to dress up the story rather, to describe our duel as a matter of life-and-death. But the fact of the matter was that we both arrived at the scene so full of devil water we could barely hold our weapons. Whereupon we fell about in great laughter and slept the afternoon right where our seconds left us, propped up against an old sequoia tree.

On my lecture tours I learnt that I could win the attention of my audiences by first gripping them with the excitement of the impending duel, describing in grisly detail the damage our weapons might inflict, and then endearing them to me by revealing the hilarious nature of the event. They would always leave my lectures feeling they had gotten good value for their dime.

Young Henry Appleton, however, was a different kettle of fish. It transpired that while he enjoyed my adventure stories, and had read all my books to that date, he was not interested in hearing about my exploits. He wanted to learn the trade of the writer.

His first knock at the door of my hotel room was timid. Expecting a servant to enter with refreshments, I called, "Be not faint-hearted lest the devil take yer throat!"

Henry entered carrying not a bottle of whiskey but my own work, *'Wild Bill and the Indian outlaw'*, which of course I appreciated. But when I suggested he should attend my lecture that very evening, he explained that his mother would disapprove. His mother! This was hardly the mark of an independent and rebellious young man, and certainly not the mark of an adventurer. However I have never subscribed to the view that a hero is one who feels no fear. A true hero to me is someone who experiences real fear and yet persists with his dangerous mission.

This is why I have no hesitation in calling Henry Appleton a hero.

However I had not yet discerned the heart of this young man who stumbled into my darkened room, and therefore had some fun at his expense.

"Sonny," I said, "some of the most feared outlaws of the Wild West are half your age."

Seeing the disdain with which he viewed my drinking, I delivered with great gusto a line I had borrowed from the Indians: *In every bottle there is one song and a hundred fights.* The Indians are great storytellers, and over the years I have made many of their tales my own.

But I could see young Henry was less than impressed, and I returned to his question.

"So you're a wannabe writer. Well then – 'Once upon a time ... '?"

Perhaps this was cruel. How many young people, in the presence of a legendary writer such as myself, could immediately weave a tale to command the attention of a reader? Henry was not the first aspiring writer upon whom I had placed this challenge, and many of them simply dried up and fled in embarrassment.

This humble scribe is honest enough to confess that he requires a sip of two of whiskey to fuel his imagination. But Henry, as sober as a County judge at a hanging, was quick to jump in and begin his tale.

"Once upon a time," he said, "there was a fatherless young man, desperate to save the family farm. So he decided to rob a bank."

And there you have it. In two sentences, a story outline worthy of an accomplished novelist and one sure to win the ear of an adventure-hungry young reader.

"Great start, kid," I told him.

"Has this young man got a gun?"

"Yes, sir. He's going to steal his father's rifle."

Steal his father's gun?! Swell, I thought, and took a sip of whiskey. In my mind's notebook I recorded this idea, to be included in my next novel.

The young man was not finished.

"I can draw, too, sir."

He handed over several sheets of paper decorated top to bottom with sketches of cowboys embroiled in battles with marauding Indians.

"Not half bad, kid," I said. In truth, his pictures were as good as most which graced my novels, but I felt it my duty to discourage him from pursuing a career as whiskey-soaked and fickle as mine. So I gave him a spoonful of honest advice.

"You know these yarns are mostly baloney, don'tcha kid. Most of those so-called Wild West heroes are just ornery jerks like you and me. Ceptin' they're stupid enough to get a gun an' start shootin' folks."

I hesitated to burden this young man with the heavy truth, but I felt he needed to hear it.

"They mostly die young, Henry. Their flesh ripped apart by pieces of lead."

I had seen it all. Cocky young cowhands, boasting leather jackets with tassels, and waving pistols mint fresh from the store, dropped stone cold dead by a single bullet from the revolver of a heartless gunslinger. Young adventurers who had hoped the whole country would ring with their fame, instead left in the dust to be claimed by a weeping mother or lover.

Henry asked why I continued to write about them. In answering, I was more honest than I usually had cause to be.

"It is a livin'," I replied. "A very respectable livin'."

Indeed, my books had paid for my whiskey and lodgings around the world, from New York to New Zealand, and I had no reason to complain.

I looked at this young man, handsome in face and form, and clearly marked out for worthy deeds. I knew from the cut of his figure and the honesty blazing in his eyes that he had heart and resolve. It came as no surprise when, within weeks, I learned how he had stood up to the fiendish Richard Burgess and his gang.

"Sorry to knock the wind outa ya sails, kid," I continued. "But folks buy these books 'cos they're desperate for heroes. To brighten up their own dull lives."

Then I gave this promising man some advice which I believe, without boasting, that he took to heart.

"Best advice I can give ya, kid..." I said. "Don't write about other people. Write your own story. And live it."

The Good Lord knows I often wish I had taken my own advice. But I continued to live in the shadow of men more brave or reckless by far, and earnt a good living by writing about them and their life-risking escapades.

"Live it," I repeated. "Seek your own course. Mark out your own path."

As he left the room, a thought passed through my mind:

"One day, Henry Appleton, if you follow your own path, someone will write your story."

And so it came to pass, within the covers of the very book which now rests in your hands.

SEVENTEEN
A FATEFUL MEETING

JUNE THE 10TH, 1866 WAS THE DATE OF AN HISTORIC meeting. Not between the leaders of two great nations, nor between the chiefs of two legendary Indian tribes. It was the day goodness in the form of Henry Appleton met evil in the form of Richard Burgess, oft-convicted criminal, many times a murderer, a man who openly called himself "a true disciple of my cruel master Satan."

Henry's mother gave him a basket containing eggs and other produce from their garden, with instructions to give them to Dr Smith, and Henry set off on Duke.

He enjoyed his daily trek to Nelson. Sitting straight in the saddle of his beloved Duke, just like his heroes, the lawmen of the American West, and trotting through beautiful countryside.

He travelled at a leisurely pace across the familiar landscape, determined to enjoy the day and avoid the glares of Chadwick and Dodge at the bank. But when he spied two strangers a short distance ahead of him, sitting by a camp fire, he pulled sharply on the reins.

Both strangers were muddied and unkempt, like so many of the drifters who trudged along the forest tracks linking the small settlements around here. But Henry, who was a good judge of character, could tell at a glance that these two men were different, and he had no wish to engage in conversation with them.

The bigger man had a soulless face which could have been chiselled out of rock. He was squatting on his large, dirty work boots and grinding a knife on a stone.

Next to him, a smaller man flicked the leaves off his velvet-and-silk waistcoat with shaking hands.

"This is the most dirty, horrible, unforgiving, God-forsaken place since the creation of Adam," he snivelled.

"Kelly, shut yer cake hole, ya dandy," said the big man in an Irish brogue. "And stop jitterin'."

The smaller man – the 'dandy' – replied, also in an Irish brogue.

"Aye aye Sullivan."

He could not stop his hands trembling, so he tucked them in his pockets. As he did so, Henry caught a glimpse of the tattoo of a mermaid above his wrist.

Henry pulled Duke's reins firmly, to coax him away, and Duke snorted in protest. At this, both men looked up and saw Henry. They tensed.

The big man, Sullivan, rose slowly to his feet, the knife held behind his back.

And as Henry so often reasoned, he reasoned now that he should have a gun. "I should have a gun," he muttered as he entered the forest.

Of course Henry did not know it at the time, but he had just made the acquaintance of two members of the notorious Burgess gang, Joseph Sullivan and Thomas Kelly, and he was about to meet another.

Without warning a squat, muscular man stepped out in front of him.

Duke was just as surprised as Henry, and reared. The basket flew in the air, and Henry tumbled to the ground, winded. Precious vegetables scattered everywhere.

The man grabbed the reins and restrained Duke. Henry sat up, moaning, and looked up at him.

The man was bald, with bushy moustache and side chops. He too was muddy. His clothes had been slept in. But he had a commanding presence.

"If it ain't Henry Appleton!" he said.

Henry's jaw dropped.

The basket flew in the air, and Henry
tumbled to the ground, winded

"Yeah, I know who youse are, kid. Done me 'omework."

He spoke in the Cockney accent that Henry recognized from his short life in England.

He held out a hand.

"Richard Burgess."

Burgess hauled Henry to his feet.

"Here ya go, lad. Now 'Enry, I got some questions—"

Henry spotted the pistol in Burgess's belt, and despite his fear he leaned closer for a look.

Burgess winked, conspiratorial, and flicked open his coat to allow Henry a good view of the pistol.

It was not shiny, like his father's rifle, or Doctor Smith's, or the Sergeant's. But it was a weapon, and Henry did not own one.

"For protection, laddie," said Burgess. "A man needs a gun."

Henry crawled around picking up the vegetables that had survived. The tomatoes had exploded when they hit the ground. Burgess handed him the one egg that had survived the fall.

"A good omen, yeah? Heh heh."

"Who's this then?"

Henry looked up to see a pair of dirty working boots in the shadows. It was the Irishman with the hard face. Sullivan.

"Why's he snoopin' round here, then?"

He cracked his knuckles.

Another man appeared from the shadows, puffing. Henry's fear intensified as he realised there were four men in this group. His heart was pounding. Here he was, a slim young man surrounded by four grown men of dubious character.

The new arrival was tall and bony, like Sullivan, but nowhere near as powerfully built. He dressed like a businessman.

"Levy! Welcome back!" cried Burgess. "What news?"

Levy's darting eyes fixed on Henry. He spoke in an educated but reedy voice – and took care with his words.

"They – ah – the 'party' we're expecting will be here day after tomorrow."

Sullivan reacted to this.

"We got work to do. Stop pissin' around, Burgess."

Burgess ignored him, and Sullivan retreated into the bushes with Kelly and Levy. Burgess handed the basket to Henry.

" 'Ere you are lad. Your muvver'll want this."

He helped Henry pick up a few carrots.

"Your muvver's name's Victoria, innit."

Henry's mouth hung open. But he dared not ask.

Burgess hoisted Henry onto Duke.

"Thank you – sir."

Henry nudged Duke. But the horse did not move: Burgess was still holding the reins.

"I'm guessin' you 'ave a job in town. Eh, 'Enry?"

"Yes, sir, the bank ..."

The moment he had spoken, he regretted it.

EIGHTEEN
IF I HAD A GUN!

"The bank, eh?" said Burgess.

Henry thoughts began running around like startled chickens in his brain, as he tried to think of a clever escape plan. Perhaps he would jump off Duke's back and set off on foot, running as fast as he could, and then further down the path he would whistle his special whistle and Duke would trot after him? Henry snorted at his own ridiculous idea: he could never rely on Duke.

What should he do?

"Burgess!" Sullivan barked. "Let's be awf!"

Burgess released Duke's bridle.

"We'll talk soon, kid. Now git!"

He whacked Duke's rump, and the horse took off.

Henry looked back to see Sullivan, Kelly and Levy

hurriedly dousing their camp fire. There was no sign of Burgess.

Henry cantered through the forest, shaking from his encounter. He was always on edge beneath these giant trees which cast such dark shadows, but today was worse. Duke seemed skittish too. Even the birds had fallen silent.

He pulled Duke to a stop, and leant forward to catch his breath.

"It's all right, Duke," he tried to calm his horse. But they both jumped when they heard the *snap* of a branch.

Henry looked around, and tried to ignore the flickering shapes in the undergrowth. He knew there were no dangerous animals in New Zealand – apart from the occasional wild pigs, and they usually kept their distance.

"Git!"

He kicked Duke into action. They picked their way through the tangle of roots and shrubs on the forest floor, thankful that some hardy soul had hacked away the long trails of supplejack vines which hung in loops from the trees.

As he continued his journey, he pondered his own life and his mother's unhappiness. And those four strangers – what did they want?

He emerged from the forest and stepped into the clearing with its cemetery and chapel. The place was deserted, but strangely comforting. Henry slumped in the saddle.

"Why are my hands shaking?" he asked out loud.

He looked back at the forest: dark and brooding. He imagined it was inviting him – daring him – to step back inside its leafy cathedral.

In front of the Celtic cross which marked his father's grave, Henry knelt.

"Father," he began.

He often talked to his father, and told him what was racing around in his head.

He didn't feel proud of the way he had reacted to the sinister men in the forest. Wild Bill Hickok wouldn't have been afraid. But then, Wild Bill always carried a knife. And a rifle. And Henry had neither.

He shut his eyes and asked God to make him a man. Was that too much to ask? He opened his eyes and peered at his father's headstone: 'correct oppression; bring justice to the fatherless.'

Henry screwed up his face. He recalled the school-room incident when he had stood up to Jasper Thornton in order to 'correct oppression", and Jasper had knocked him clean off his feet.

Henry shook his head to stop the daydreaming, and stood up.

A twig snapped and he turned around.

Standing there, next to Duke, was Richard Burgess.

NINETEEN
THE OUTLAW'S INVITATION

HENRY'S FIRST REACTION WAS OF COURSE ONE OF FEAR: HE thought he had escaped after his encounter with the gang: and now he was confronted again by one of the scariest men he had ever met. But his second thought was – how did this man make the journey through the bushes so quickly, on foot?

Burgess's chest was heaving.

"I'm a tough old rooster, 'Enry," he grinned. He paused for breath.

"Years ov livin' on the road."

He took several deep breaths before signalling Henry to come closer.

"It is not a bad life, y'know."

He laid a calloused hand on Henry's shoulder.

"Master of yer own destiny."

Henry backed away, but Burgess continued his lecture.

"You 'eard of Robin 'ood, laddie?"

"Robin Hood? Yes, sir. He robbed from the rich to give to the poor."

Every English schoolboy had read stories about Robin Hood and his Merry Men. His adventures were almost as exciting as those of the Wild West, although Henry preferred cowboys because they had guns, not bows and arrows.

Burgess grinned.

"Well that's us. Robbin' the rich to 'elp the poor."

Henry blinked: this brutish, muddy man was nothing like Robin Hood, who was surely a slim, handsome, youthful figure dressed elegantly in forest green.

"You like that notion, don'tcha?" Burgess enthused. "I can see you're a man of integrity. Like yours truly. We're men of principle."

Henry wanted to laugh out loud at this preposterous notion, but he kept his mouth firmly shut.

"I look after me friends. Loyalty, 'Enry, loyalty."

Burgess place his hand on Duke's saddle. He was holding his pistol, and Henry couldn't take his eyes off it.

"You an' me gunna do some good work togevva, 'Enry."

Henry shuddered at the thought.

"Meantime..."

Burgess shoved his face close to Henry's.

"Meantime, don't tell nobody 'bout us, all right. Know what I mean?"

"No," trembled Henry. "I mean – yes. Yes, sir."

He was still looking at the pistol, and Burgess shoved the weapon into Henry's hands.

" 'Ere. 'ave an' 'old. Ain't she sweet?"

Henry, wide-eyed, ran his fingers along the barrel.

"A fing of great beauty in design an' mechanics, innit?" Burgess purred. "So pretty, but then—

"BAM!"

Burgess made the sound so loud and percussive that it could have been a gunshot. Henry jumped.

"Jus' like that, 'Enry, ya can send a man to 'is Maker. Know what I mean?"

Burgess took back the pistol, chuckling. Then, like a panther, he sprang onto Duke. Henry had read many accounts of cowboys leaping onto their horses this way – but they were just stories. He had never believed it possible until he saw Burgess do it.

Burgess saw Henry's disbelief and chuckled as he

stroked Duke's neck with a firm hand. "Been a while since I 'ad an 'orse," he said. "Back in Australia – me 'n' me mates used to travel 'undreds o' miles in a day." He turned in the saddle to grin. Henry saw the man's dirty and broken teeth.

"We'd borrow a nag, ride 'im 'ard for sixty miles, then trade 'im in for fresh legs at the next station."

Henry sniffed. "You mean you stole them."

"Nah, just swapped 'em," said Burgess. "No 'arm done."

He reached down and held out a hand.

"Now come on, son. I'll give youse a lift into town."

Henry wished he could find the words – and the courage – to object. "This is my horse!" he thought. "How dare you act as if you own him?" But he said nothing, and allowed Burgess to haul him up onto the saddle behind him.

And as they sauntered across the landscape – Burgess was in no hurry – Henry realised that he was quite enjoying Burgess's company. He had some exciting yarns to tell.

"Life on the road, 'Enry, life on the road. Master of yer own destiny. Beholden to nobody."

Henry could imagine it. No chores. No digging the garden. Just a free and easy life on the road, sleeping under the stars. And being respected by law-abiding folk.

Henry knew he was in the presence of a bona fide outlaw. He wondered whether Burgess had actually killed a man. He was quite sure he had. Burgess had hinted as much. Probably many men.

They reached the edge of town and Burgess slipped to the ground. He walked a few paces before turning to face Henry.

"An' 'Enry, I'm invitin' youse to come join us," he said. "Join the Burgess Gang." He delivered the invitation in a matter-of-fact way, and Henry knew he meant it.

"Howzat, eh? You an' me – jus' like Robin 'ood."

Burgess walked off without waiting for an answer, but the way Henry was feeling right now he would probably have said "Yes, sir! I will join your gang, I will!"

Henry shifted in the saddle, watching Burgess with a mixture of fear and admiration. Burgess disappeared behind a building.

What an honour, Henry thought. Here he was, the same age as some of the most feared outlaws in America, being asked to become part of a fearsome gang in New Zealand.

He could see himself standing side by side with the

mighty Sullivan, inviting anyone to challenge them. Fearless. And armed, all of them.

Henry Appleton with his own pistol. What would his mother think of that?

He trotted into the main street of Nelson, head held high.

TWENTY
REVELATIONS

"I've been invited to join a real gang," thought Henry as he tied up his horse outside the Trafalgar, his hands trembling with excitement. Certainly there would be blood spilt, but Robin Hood also took lives when necessary.

Henry continued to debate Burgess's offer as he bounded up the stairs of the hotel and knocked on Smith's door.

He was quite unprepared for what happened next.

A light voice answered: "Who is it?"

Henry was taken aback: it sounded like a girl's voice.

"It is me – Henry. Is Dr Smith there?"

The door opened a crack. Eyes scanned Henry, then moved away. The door remained ajar, so Henry nudged it open.

The room had been divided in half by a semi-opaque curtain, strung up from wall to wall on a piece of twine. Through the gauze Henry could see the shape of Rama, wearing a cap and baggy jacket, standing at the basin, scrubbing clothes.

Henry perched on a chair, and got out his dime novel. It seemed rude not to talk to the person who was in the same room, only a few feet away, so he called out:

"You'll never guess who I met."

He decided not to spill the beans about his encounter with Burgess. There was a little niggle in his head that suggested that would not be a good idea.

"Johnny Slick!"

Henry waved his dime novel in the direction of the curtain.

"The man who writes these cowboy stories. He's amazing."

There was a muffled response. The sound of running water. Henry wandered to the window and saw Doctor Smith striding towards the hotel. He opened the window to call out.

As he did so, a breeze entered the room, ruffling the partition curtain, and for a few seconds a gap allowed Henry a clear view of Rama.

Rama was bent over the basin, sleeves rolled up,

revealing bare arms. They were slender and smooth. The hands were delicate.

As Rama looked up, Henry saw the face clearly for the first time. The eyes were soft, gentle. With a shake of the head, Rama released a cascade of long dark hair.

All these images Henry took in fleetingly, as the curtain billowed open. His jaw dropped as it dawned on him – *Rama is a girl!* A young woman his own age!

This set Henry's young heart racing. He blushed and turned to close the window. The curtain settled, and Rama was once more just a diffused shape behind the curtain.

Henry sat and fidgeted.

He picked up the dime novel. Stared at it. Put it away. Looked at the ceiling. He started to hum, then hopped up to look out the window again. Studied the clouds.

"Henry!"

Henry started. Doctor Smith was in the room.

"Time to pay our respects to the Sergeant. Come."

Henry scrambled to follow him. And as Smith marched ahead of him up Bridge Street, Henry ventured to glance back at the hotel window. He was strangely excited to see Rama there, looking down at him.

Visions of this young woman, his own age, displaced Richard Burgess from Henry's thoughts for a while. But not for long. As he sat in Sergeant Nash's office listening to Dr Smith, a dark picture emerged of Burgess and his gang. A picture of treachery and murder. The good doctor told them how his young wife had been murdered in Australia two years ago, and he believed Richard Burgess was the killer.

Dr Smith was carrying with him a bloody finger-print which he claimed would identify the killer. The murderer had placed his bloodied hand on a piece of furniture in the doctor's home as he fled, leaving "a unique signature".

"He murdered her!?"

"Yes, Henry," said Smith. "These men are cold blooded killers."

Henry was thinking, of course, of Burgess and Sullivan. These men were parading as romantic adventurers, but Henry realised they were most likely the same men in Smith's bloody nightmare.

"Sergeant," the doctor said, "I believe these men are now right here in your district."

"How so?"

"I tracked a gang of London criminals from Sydney to Hokitika. They were chased out of the West Coast suspected of armed robbery and murder, and headed north."

Smith nodded towards the hills.

"The gang was travelling in this direction. And one of them is the killer."

"And he'll face the gallows, to be sure," replied Sergeant Nash.

Smith looked straight at the Sergeant.

"I plan to apprehend him myself."

The Sergeant got to his feet.

"Doctor Smith, sir – we certainly need good men who are willing to stand up for Law and Order. But taking the Law into their own hands? No."

Smith stared at Sergeant Nash.

Sergeant Nash stared back.

Henry's mind was spinning. He was certain now that his menacing friends from the forest were not the romantic Robin Hood characters they made themselves out to be, but a fearsome gang. And he could not stand by and let them continue on their murdering way.

So he stepped forward and declared:

"I've seen them!"

All eyes turned to Henry.

"The men you're looking for. I know where they are!"

TWENTY-ONE
BACK INTO THE HILLS

Henry led Dr Smith and Rama up into the Maungatapu hills that he knew so well. They galloped into the fields, past the chapel and into the forest.

When they reached Pritchard's Glade, Henry became unsettled. He wondered whether he was doing the right thing. The situation was bound to get worse, and he would be right at the centre of it all. Sergeant Nash had declined to join them, as no crime had been committed, and he had urged Smith not to go – but this did not deter the physician.

Finally they reached the spot where Henry had been ambushed by Burgess.

Rama slipped from her horse to study the ground.

"The fire's over there," Henry told them.

Smith dismounted and walked carefully to the campfire embers, while Rama examined the ground.

"Four men," she said with certainty.

Smith wasted no time in checking near the Maungatapu Rock. He was certain that his quarry – the gang he had tracked from Australia to various parts of New Zealand over the past two years – had never been closer.

While Smith was searching for any sign of the gang, Henry was left with Rama. They talked about the doctor's obsession with finding the man who killed his wife. They talked about Rama's parents – her mother had died, her father had gone back to England. They talked about the measles and influenza, introduced by European immigrants, that had claimed the lives of so many members of her family. And finally Henry plucked up the courage to ask:

"Why do you pretend to be a man?"

"It saves a lot of questions," she said.

Henry frowned. He had seen how some of the young women in Nelson led miserable lives, working as servants, and how they were often mistreated by the ruffians who frequented the bars. But he was the kind of young man who liked to have all the answers, so he opened his mouth to ask another question.

Rama stopped him.

"Henry," she said quietly. "You are a good man. Please tell no-one."

Henry swallowed his questions and nodded.

She laid a hand on his wrist. "Thank you."

Henry had just one question he needed to ask.

"Rama – is that your real name?"

"It is Miriama," she said. "Drop of the sea."

"That's a beautiful name," he said.

She smiled.

But there was a different name on the doctor's lips.

Burgess.

When they returned to Smith's hotel room, the doctor challenged Henry to make a sketch of Richard Burgess. He was pleased with the result.

"I trust my instincts," he said, "and my instincts tell me Burgess is the man who killed my wife."

Then he asked Henry to sketch Burgess's accomplice Sullivan, and watched him keenly.

"You have good hands."

"Thank you sir," said Henry. "I would like to be an illustrator like Johnny Slick."

Smith took Henry's drawing of Sullivan, and examined it.

"Excellent. Now our friend the Sergeant will have to act."

Once again Doctor Smith hurried from the hotel,

this time clasping Henry's sketches, and once again he marched up Bridge Street to the Sergeant's office. Henry followed with Duke, tethered the horse and went to a side window to peer in.

Smith laid Henry's sketches on the Sergeant's desk with a dramatic flourish. "These are the men I told you about," he said.

Sergeant Nash looked closely.

"They are good sketches, Doctor Smith. But these men have committed no crime that I know of."

"So what do you propose?" demanded Smith.

Sergeant Nash spread his hands.

"I have sent a letter to the Police in Sydney for details of their investigation into your wife's death."

"A letter! That will take weeks," Smith fumed.

"Doctor, I cannot send deputies into the hills looking for men who have not committed a crime here. If they come into town we'll keep a watch on them."

The Sergeant stood.

"Meanwhile, Doctor, please – do not be tempted to take the Law into your own hands."

Smith had heard enough. He turned and marched out. Henry and Miriama were waiting.

"You heard that?" The doctor's face was flushed. "Some thug murdered my beautiful wife – and I'm told to be patient."

Miriama placed a hand on Smith's arm, but he pulled away. "He must face justice."

Henry stared at Smith. He saw for the first time a man consumed with the desire for revenge.

"I won't give up until his blood is spilt just like Alicia's," Smith declared.

This shocked Henry.

"Sir – you said you would deliver him to the Sergeant! Not *kill* him!"

Smith looked at him, blank.

"You're too young to understand," he said.

Henry hated the way adults could so easily dismiss someone like him, as if he didn't know the difference between right and wrong.

"Dr Smith wants to be judge and executioner," he said to Miriama as Smith strode away.

Miriama nodded sadly. "The Chinese have a proverb," she said. "Before embarking on a journey of revenge, prepare two graves."

She pulled her coat around her, and ran after Smith. Henry watched, powerless to stop either of them.

He saw Miriama catch up with Smith, and walk a few paces behind him. She took a quick glance back at Henry. He raised his hand to wave, but too late.

Smith and Miriama left the street and disappeared around the corner.

TWENTY-TWO
HENRY SAVES THE BANKER

THE SUN WAS DIPPING BEHIND THE TWO-STOREY WOODEN buildings that lined Bridge Street as Henry set off for home. Being cautious by nature, it was his habit where practical to steer Duke to the centre of the road, thus keeping out of reach of any man whose heart was as black as the shadows.

So it was that, approaching the bank where he worked, Henry was dismayed to see the bulky shape of Mr Lester J. Chadwick emerge from the blackness. Henry had no desire to speak to this man, who had put *Auction – Mortgagee Sale* notices on at least half a dozen settlers' cottages besides the Appletons' own. The bank manager caught his eye and Henry was compelled to acknowledge him, but Chadwick did not respond. He shoved a bulky collection of keys in his coat pocket and headed off down the street.

Henry gave his steed a firm nudge and trotted ahead of Chadwick, determined to reach the end of the street before him. However he had not proceeded more than a dozen yards when he saw, protruding from a dark doorway, a pair of familiar boots.

They were the unmistakeable boots of Satan's henchman, Joseph Sullivan.

Henry made a decision as fast as the human eye reacts to a spark that spits from the campfire, and resolved to continue his journey without paying any attention to the lurking bushranger. He turned at the next street corner, and then quickly dismounted, setting off on foot to follow Sullivan who had now fallen in behind Chadwick, maintaining a cautious distance and keeping well hidden in the shadows.

The three of them presented an odd sight as they crossed the open ground behind the shops and offices of Nelson: a large and out-of-breath bank manager, followed by an even larger ruffian whose light step belied his size, and a stone's throw behind them the slight figure of Henry Appleton. The bank manager was oblivious to any danger, and the ruffian was filled with nothing but malice.

Young Henry's heart was ice as he contemplated

what evil Sullivan might carry out. He considered it possible that Sullivan had a pistol concealed beneath his jacket, but his mode of murder could well be more simple yet just as ugly, for it was known that Sullivan was once a pugilist whose fist could stop a man's heart with one blow.

Henry kept his distance as Chadwick entered his neat cottage and Sullivan took up a position behind the bushes near the front door. A lantern came on in the front window, and as he saw Sullivan take a step out of the darkness, Henry made his move. He strode boldly across the street, whistling loud enough to startle the birds.

Sullivan retreated into the darkness again as Henry mounted the front steps and rapped firmly on Chadwick's door. He was close enough to the hidden monster to hear the breath rattling in his great chest.

The bank manager opened his door cautiously, and Henry gave him no time to protest, pushing his way inside and shutting the door firmly behind him.

"Sir, I am sorry," Henry began, ever the polite son, "but outside your front door is a man who wishes you great harm. I believe he has followed you with the intent of taking ownership of the keys to the bank."

The bank manager set his eyes upon the keys he had just placed on the table.

"Good Lord!"

Without further word he approached a cupboard in the hallway and produced a shotgun: a weapon Henry had never had the opportunity to handle.

"Take this!" wheezed Chadwick, loading the weapon before thrusting it into Henry's arms. With that, Henry found himself being marched down the hallway and pushed out the back door.

Chadwick hid behind the young man, who, realising he must now concentrate his attention on Sullivan rather than the man cowering behind him, raised the shotgun to his chest. Already he had a plan. He would approach Sullivan from behind and use the advantage of surprise to capture him. But his plan was dashed when Chadwick yelled "Come out, whoever you are!"

Henry prepared to fire his weapon at the big man as he sprang from the bushes. But he did not appear.

"He has made off," he told Chadwick. His voice was calm but his heart was in tumult. He knew he had just used another of the proverbial cat's nine lives.

With any immediate danger gone, Chadwick was now bold enough to step out from behind Henry. His forehead glistened with sweat, and his hands were so clammy the gun nearly slipped from his hands as he took it back from Henry.

Henry looked around at the houses, the bushes, the

shadows. Sullivan might well be there, still dangerous, and eager for an opportunity to avenge himself on the young man who had just thwarted his plans.

Henry mustered all his strength and sprinted back towards the shops and the company of his faithful horse Duke.

Henry prepared to fire his weapon at
Sullivan as he sprang from the bushes

TWENTY-THREE
'I AM YOUR FATHER'

Henry and Duke galloped home across the darkening landscape, past the chapel and graveyard, and through the forest. Finally they reached the comforting sight of Bluebell Cottage with the glow of a lantern in its window and a wisp of smoke from the chimney.

As he unsaddled Duke, Henry heard the haunting notes of *Fur Elise*, a tune his mother often played as she sat at her faithful old piano which they had shipped all the way from England.

But when he heard the notes stumble, he knew something was wrong. And moments later his worst fears were confirmed as the hateful figure of Richard Burgess appeared at the door.

Henry's mother ran out, shaking with fear, and our young hero stood to her defence.

"What are you doing here?" he demanded of Burgess.

"A man needs a woman's company from time to time," Burgess said, leering. At this, Henry cried out – and charged.

This was not a wise course of action, as Burgess was a much stronger man whose muscular body had been hardened by years of prison service and life on the roads of Australia and New Zealand. But Henry did not give this a thought, and threw himself against Burgess with all his strength. They both crashed back inside the cottage, sending furniture flying and crockery smashing.

Henry's mother rushed inside, to find her son already overpowered by the bushranger. Neither the boy nor his mother were to know that this man had killed perhaps two dozen men for financial gain. But Burgess admired the courage of friend or foe alike. He had once set a trooper free when the man refused at gunpoint to get off his horse and submit to Burgess's demands. And now, Burgess demonstrated that same admiration for the young man who had just, foolishly, attempted to overpower him.

He put Henry in a choke hold, but stopped short of applying enough pressure to end the young man's life.

"Tell him to quit!" he yelled.

Henry's mother screamed:

"Henry – please! Stop!"

Henry, his face red, stopped kicking. He was gasping like a fish.

Burgess loosened his grip.

"You're a plucky li'l squirt. But ya need to pick yer fights, sonny. I coulda burked ya, easy."

Burgess addressed Henry's mother, backed against the wall.

"I were an 'othead like 'im when I were a boy."

"A hothead? Henry's a better man than you'll ever be."

"I should hope so," Burgess replied. "Me own muvva didn't know what to do wiv me."

He stared into space, and made a comment Henry would remember forever.

"Fink I was born a devil," he said.

He hauled Henry to his feet.

"Both ov you – sit."

Mother and son put the table and chairs back in place and sat down, hand in hand. It was clear Burgess had an announcement to make, but first he wanted to tell them a story.

"I recall," he began, "when I were 'bout your age, 'Enry. I were just comin' out of the slammer. You know – prison. And there at the gates, waiting for me, were me two best friends in the world – me sweet muvva, and me sister Emma. And on the uvver side of the road, me mates, come to claim me back as one of their own."

He chuckled. "I were a pickpocket back then, 'Enry – one of the best."

Henry's mother had heard enough.

"What's this got to do with—"

Burgess silenced her with an upraised hand. He waited to make sure she wasn't going to talk again before continuing.

"Me muvva and me sister pleaded wiv me, they did. 'Renounce your ways. Choose the God-fearin' path'."

Burgess nodded at Henry.

"She were a God-fearin' woman, 'Enry, just like your mum."

He grinned. "Course, I didn't 'renounce me ways', did I. I chose the path of evil instead."

Burgess took out his pistol and placed it on the table in front of him. Henry wondered if he should grab it and attempt an escape. But Burgess laid a hand on the weapon, and his dark eyes drilled into Henry's.

"Now," he said. "Some personal business."

The bushranger reached into his jacket and brought out a piece of paper which he had clearly been carrying around for some time. It was yellowed, dirty and crumpled. He spread it out on the table and attempted to flatten it smooth.

He spoke slowly and deliberately.

"Mrs Appleton. Victoria. Your boy – 'Enry here. He's adopted, right? You know that, don'tcha lad?"

"Of course I know," said Henry, putting his hand on his mother's. "This is my mother now."

"Yeah, yeah. Shut up kid."

Burgess pointed at the document. "An' he was born in London, right?"

They waited ...

"On April the 26th, 1851, yeah?"

He paused. "I'll cut to the chase, 'Enry."

Those dark eyes fixed on Henry again.

"I'm ya farver."

"What?" cried the young man in disbelief.

"I'm yer farver," Burgess repeated. "Your Papa. Daddy."

Henry gasped.

"You're not! You can't be!"

He sprang to his feet.

"Mother?"

Henry appealed to his mother, but she said nothing, and glanced at the photo of her husband on the wall. She took Henry's arm and talked directly to Burgess.

"What was the name of your – lady friend?" she asked.

"Says it 'ere." Burgess poked a finger at the document. "Lizzie. Lizzie Sprickle." There was a hint of genuine affection in his voice.

"Describe her?"

"Short, pretty – much like yerself, Missus. Blazin' eyes."

"Where did she live?"

"Foster's Lane. Number 12. Upstairs."

"What was her trade?"

"Seamstress."

Henry's mother fell silent. He stared at her, waiting.

"I never saw me kid," said Burgess. "Day after Lizzie told me she had a sprog in the oven, I were shipped off to Australia."

He stabbed the paper.

"Look at this – 'farver unknown'. Huh!"

He sat back, reflective.

"I never saw Lizzie after that. Or me kid."

He gave Henry a playful punch.

"Till now, yeah?"

Henry had always known he was adopted, and sometimes imagined he would one day meet his birth parents. But he could not contemplate the thought that his father would be this monster of a man.

His mother put a hand on Henry's arm and spoke slowly, carefully.

"Your natural mother was a seamstress, Henry. And her name was Lizzie."

"Someone must have told him!" Henry protested.

Burgess tapped the birth certificate.

"It's all 'ere, son."

Burgess had finished delivering his big news. Now he picked up his pistol and pushed Henry outside, kicking the door shut behind them.

TWENTY-FOUR
A ROBIN HOOD PLAN

BURGESS POINTED AT THE *AUCTION SOON* SIGN THE BANK manager had nailed to the front gate.

"You and yer muvva, you're in big strife, lad," he said. "The bank's gunna sell yer farm right from under yer feet. You. Are. Screwed."

He put an arm around Henry.

"Listen, son. Yer farver – the uvver one – he ain't 'ere no more. So I'm gunna take ya under me wing, right?"

"No!" Henry tried to pull away, but Burgess held him tight, and patted his cheek. Not hard, but threatening. And again, a bit harder. A slap this time.

"Quit yer squawkin', kid. I'm givin' youse a chance to help yer muvver."

He leaned close. "We're gunna play a li'l trick on your friend the banker. He's gunna 'and over his gold."

"What!?"

"Me band of merry men," Burgess laughed. "We're like Robin 'ood. Know what I mean? We're gunna take the gold and give it to the poor. And some for youse, 'Enry."

The adventures of Robin Hood and his men in green were among Henry's favourite stories. Burgess did not resemble Robin Hood in any way, but he continued with his sinister argument.

"You get to give yer own share to yer muvva, so she can buy the farm an' all."

"That's ... robbery!"

"Course it is, son. But face facts – the bank stole it from youse in the first place. We ain't doin' nuffink wrong."

This did not sit right with Henry, whose adoptive parents were upright and honest, and had taught him the Ten Commandments by the time he was six.

"Thou shall not steal!" he said firmly.

Burgess was not impressed.

"Everyfink's black an' white for you, innit? But in the real world it ain't so simple. We're simply gonna take back some of the money wot the bank stole from youse in the first place. It's a little wrong to balance out a big wrong. See? That's the diff."

Burgess pulled Henry towards him and embraced him in a crushing bear hug.

"This is a proud moment for yer old man, 'Enry."

Henry wriggled out of Burgess's arms.

"You're not my father!"

Burgess raised his hand as if to slap him, but stopped. He took a deep breath, and put his arm around Henry in a friendly fashion.

"Now 'Enry. On a nuvva matter. Me mates saw a gentleman this afternoon, riding round in them woods. Very determined, he were."

He waited. Henry said nothing, but gulped as he realised the gang had seen Dr Smith.

"You were seen wiv him, 'Enry."

Burgess straightened Henry's collar, casual but menacing.

"Who is he?" he demanded. "What's he want?"

Henry decided he must tell the truth, and blurted it out.

"He's trying to find the man who murdered his wife."

Burgess was only mildly interested.

"Someone burked his old lady? Well, dumpty-doo. And?"

Henry wondered what else he could say, when suddenly Burgess gripped Henry.

"Tomorra, get us the keys to the bank."

Burgess's eyes flicked to the side of the cottage, and Henry turned to see what had caught the man's attention. He saw nothing but shadows.

He turned back to Burgess.

"How can I get the keys? I'm not even allowed to touch them!"

"You'll find a way. Bring them to me."

"So you can rob the bank?!"

"Put it this way, 'Enry – you'll be saving lives," Burgess told him calmly. "Wiv the keys, we can sneak into the bank quiet and peaceful. No one gets shot."

With that, Burgess shoved Henry back towards the cottage.

"Meet me tomorra, son. Midday, in Pritchard's Glade. Got that? Stroke o' noon."

Henry limped towards the cottage. He took a few steps before looking back. Burgess had gone.

The cottage door opened and a shaft of light hit Henry. His mother was there, still looking shaky.

"Henry?"

He fell inside and bolted the door. She hugged him.

"That man," she said, "that man is scum."

"But that scum said he's my father. And he might be."

His mother shook her head.

"But you are not like him, Henry."

Mother and son stared at each other. Yesterday they had problems – running the farm, trying to pay the bank loan – but those problems seemed trivial now there was a murderous gang in their lives.

"It will work out," said Victoria Appleton to her son. "Everything will work out."

Then a floorboard creaked.

Henry's mother turned around and screamed.

Standing in the corner of the room was a tall, angular, terrifying man; wearing big work boots.

TWENTY-FIVE
TAKEN HOSTAGE

JOSEPH SULLIVAN CRACKED HIS KNUCKLES.

"Surprise!" he sneered. He jumped at Henry's mother, and wrapped a sinewy arm around her neck.

Henry cried out "No!"

"Hear the little rooster crow!" Sullivan raised a large fist and knocked Henry to the floor.

"That's for interferin'," he growled. He pressed a large boot against Henry on the floor. "I seen youse in town tonight, ya little runt."

Henry lay on the floor, dazed. Sullivan's punch had split the skin on his jaw, and it began to bleed. Sullivan prodded him in the ribs with his boot.

"Get us the keys for the bank, like Burgess said. Or else."

He pushed Henry's mother towards the door,

wrenched it open and dragged her outside. She looked back at Henry, still lying on the floor.

"Henry!?"

They disappeared into the darkness.

Henry struggled to get to his feet.

"Mother!"

"Just get the keys, punk," Sullivan yelled from the darkness.

Henry staggered to the door, holding his jaw, and peered out into the night. He began to follow them, then reconsidered. He shouted:

"Don't hurt her! I'll get the keys."

He closed the front door, and avoided looking at his father's photo on the wall.

"I'll get the keys somehow," he told himself. "I have to save Mother."

He waited just inside the door, trying to think of a plan.

At the fringe of the forest, Burgess and Kelly watched Sullivan drag Henry's mother towards them. He pushed past them, half carrying her. Burgess was not happy.

"You should not ov done that, Sullivan."

"I don't trust that little toad," said Sullivan.

Henry's mother looked at Burgess, pleading. He told Sullivan, "Don't harm the woman."

"Aye aye, yer majesty. Wouldn't dream ov it."

Sullivan elbowed Kelly out of the way and dragged his hostage into the forest.

Kelly and Burgess exchanged a look.

Kelly brushed his waistcoat and looked over at the cottage.

"You reckon the lad'll do it?"

"Get the keys? Course he will. He's one helluva frightened kid. C'mon."

Burgess and Kelly followed Sullivan further into the forest.

Henry carried the lantern into his bedroom, set it down, then slumped against the wall. He touched his jaw and winced. Listened for any sounds from outside.

He was frightened all right. But he reminded himself of other times he had found the courage to act: helping to thwart a bank robbery when he was only ten; sending Dead Eye Dick to prison; and standing up to Jasper Thornton. He knew he would find a way to beat Richard Burgess and his gang.

But right now his head was hurting and he was desperate for sleep.

He crawled into the lounge ... and collapsed.

Once again he dreamt of cowboys and guns and horses, although his role in the dream was not as heroic as usual. This time, he running from dark shapes that emerged from the forest: monsters with the faces of Burgess and Sullivan.

And Burgess's leering face: "I'm yer farver."

He was woken by the twittering of birds. Dawn light flickered through the window onto his face and he moaned. His real life nightmare resumed.

He pushed himself onto his knees and peered out. Cautious.

The leaves in the trees barely stirred. Duke was standing near the cottage, asleep.

Henry touched his aching jaw and tried to think of a plan. Who would help him? How could he rescue his mother? First, though, he had to escape from the cottage without being seen. The gang might still be watching from the dark forest.

He thought of Duke, sleeping out in the front yard. He needed to lure the horse around to the back of the cottage.

Duke loved carrots. So Henry crawled into the kitchen, picked the last two carrots from the vegetable basket, and crept outside to the corner of the cottage, where he could see Duke.

He broke off a piece of carrot, and hurled it at the horse.

It fell short.

He got another piece and flung it harder. The carrot

hit Duke. The horse snorted. He saw the carrot and sniffed it. Chomped it.

Henry waved his arms. Duke looked at him, blank.

"Come to me, Duke!" Henry hissed. He waved a piece of carrot in the air, and Duke ambled towards him. Henry held out the carrot. Duke took it, and munched noisily. Henry slipped a rope over Duke's neck and led him around the back of the cottage, where they couldn't be seen from the woods.

When they reached the next field, hidden by the barn, he scrambled onto Duke's back and rode him bareback, hanging onto his mane and the rope.

Henry had no idea where Burgess and his gang might be hiding, so he made as little noise as possible. Duke seemed to understand, and trod lightly along the rough track through the forest.

Most of the birds were quiet. There was only the occasional *whoo whoo* from a morepork which had been up all night hunting insects.

Henry and Duke entered Pritchard's Glade. It was deserted and eerie. Now Henry kicked his horse into a trot.

Henry's father's headstone was prominent even in the meagre moonlight, but Henry did not look at it as he trotted past.

"I must get help."

TWENTY-SIX
TROUBLE IN TOWN

MOST OF NELSON WAS STILL ASLEEP WHEN HENRY TROTTED into town.

It was June the 13th, 1866.

A lone shopkeeper was sweeping his porch, and Henry paid no attention to him, nor to the drunk man sprawled on the sidewalk. From under his hat, pulled low, the man watched Henry leap from his horse and run into the hotel.

Henry rapped on the door to Doctor Smith's room. The doctor opened it, fully dressed. Miriama was standing behind him, once more dressed as a man.

Henry pushed past them, gasping.

"They've taken my mother!"

He collapsed into a chair.

"Burgess and Sullivan. They told me to get the keys to the bank. If I don't, they'll kill her."

"These men are monsters," said Dr Smith. He turned to Miriama.

"Rama, give Henry your room key."

Smith was a military man, much like Henry himself when he was a lone scout leading a convoy of pioneers through the forest. Henry respected him for that, and watched the doctor as he swung into action.

Dr Smith hauled a bag from beneath his bed and took out an object wrapped in cloth. Despite his anguish, Henry watched closely as Smith unwrapped the cloth bundle to reveal a pair of pearl-handled pistols. Henry had never seen pistols like these, although Johnny Slick had described a pair in his novel *Gunfight on the High Plateau*.

Smith shoved a box of cartridges into the pouch on his belt. "I'll start at Pritchard's Glade."

Henry was startled. "There're four of them," he cried.

He stood up, shakily. "I'll come with you."

"No. That would give the game away."

"What if they kill you?"

"Then you'll make sure the sergeant is waiting for them in the bank." Abruptly, Smith left the room.

Henry sat down again. Miriama squeezed his hand.

They heard the doctor's footsteps retreating down the stairs.

Henry's head was spinning. "I don't like it," he said.

The streets of Nelson were still quite empty as Smith rode out of the lane from the stables. He was about to set off when Henry rushed out.

"Doctor Smith – please wait!"

"I've waited too long, Henry."

Henry placed himself directly in front of Smith and his horse. "I'm fearful for the safety of my mother."

"I'm aware of that. Please move."

Henry hung onto the horse's bit. He didn't know what else to do. The horse shied. "Your wife's already dead," Henry cried. "I don't want my mother to die too."

Smith's face was flushed. "Let go, boy!' He slapped his whip on Henry's shoulder.

Henry yelped, and released the bit. Smith charged off.

Miriama ran out. "Henry!" She pulled back his collar to see the red welt left by Smith's whip.

Henry scrambled to his feet. "We've got to stop him!"

He was about to untie Duke when an exciting thought struck him. "The rifle!"

He headed back into the hotel.

"A man needs a gun," he remembered his father

saying. "Richard Burgess said the same thing," said an annoying voice in his head. "A gun does not make you a man," came his mother's voice.

"I need a gun!" he said out loud as he bounded up the stairs and burst into Smith's room. The physician's Calisher and Terry was where he'd seen him put it, in the corner next to the wardrobe. He grabbed it and took a box of paper cartridges from the top of the wardrobe.

"This is stealing," he thought, "but I've got to have a gun! "

He raced back down the stairs. Miriama's hand went to her mouth when she saw the rifle, but she said nothing.

"I need a gun!" said Henry. As he untied Duke, he told Miriama, "Find the sergeant! Please! Tell him what's happening."

He jumped onto Duke and galloped after Smith. Miriama watched him go, and called "Take care!" in a small voice.

Miriama headed for the side door. She paid no attention to the bedraggled man still sprawled on the footpath. He got up, cracked his knuckles, and followed her.

As Miriama reached for the door handle, a huge arm wrapped around her.

"You're not going nowhere, sonny," Sullivan grunted.

Miriama cried out. Her hands clawed at Sullivan's jacket. She stamped on his foot and smashed an elbow into his midriff.

Many men would have buckled under Miriama's determined blows. But Sullivan roared like a bull and brought down the handle of his knife on Miriama's head.

She crumpled.

TWENTY-SEVEN
HENRY IS CAPTURED

THE SUNLIGHT WAS BEGINNING TO FLOOD THE FIELDS OUTSIDE Nelson when a horse and rider appeared.

Henry Appleton galloped past the chapel, gleaming in the dawn light, and plunged into the shadowy forest. He slowed to allow Duke to find his way through the undergrowth before emerging at Pritchard's Glade.

It appeared deserted.

"Doctor Smith?" he called. He walked his horse around the perimeter, peering into the shadows, before coming to a stop in front of the cottage. The *Auction* sign hung by a nail, and a loose window creaked.

"Doctor Smith?" Henry called out. His voice was shaky.

A pigeon flapped away with heavy beats of its wings.

"Where is he?" Henry wondered. "He left town before me, so he must be here somewhere. Unless..."

Henry looked across at the other side of the glade. "Of course – he's gone to the rock."

He turned his horse, ready to resume his search, when *crack!* A twig snapped in the bushes to the right of the cottage.

"Who's there?" cried Henry. He fumbled to reach the physician's rifle which he had slung across his shoulder. As he did so, Burgess leapt out and yanked the horse's reins.

Duke reared up, and Henry tumbled off.

Agh! He landed with a thump on his back, and lay where he fell, gasping for air.

Burgess snorted. "Ya need some ridin' lessons, 'Enry."

Henry moaned and reached for the rifle on the ground. But Kelly emerged from the ferns and grabbed it.

"It's not even loaded!" he mocked.

Burgess reached into Henry's coat pocket and pulled out the box of cartridges.

"Stupid kid!" he snorted. "You ain't ready to handle no gun."

Burgess handed the cartridges to Kelly. "'ide the 'orse," he ordered.

Henry spluttered as Kelly led Duke away into the bushes.

Burgess hauled Henry to his feet and held him tight by the collar of his jacket. "You wasn't meant to come till noon," he said.

"Now I'm in trouble," thought Henry.

"Ah – I've got the key," he said. He pulled Miriama's hotel key from his pocket. Burgess grabbed it, frowning.

"The bank?"

Henry nodded.

"Eh? 'Ow come? The bank ain't open yet."

"I went in early," said Henry.

Burgess eyeballed Henry, suspicious. "Youse wouldn't dice wiv yer muvva's neck, would ya, kid?"

"No, no," Henry assured him. But he couldn't help thinking, "I hope I haven't made things worse for Mother."

"Master! Someone's comin'!" hissed Kelly from under the trees. Burgess yanked Henry into the ferns, and shoved him to the ground. Then he knelt astride him, with one hand gripped tight across his mouth.

He glared at Henry and drew his hand across his neck. The message was clear: make a noise and I'll slit your throat.

Henry spluttered and fought for breath. He heard a

horse snort as it approached the cottage, and screwed his head to one side. Through the ferns he could see the legs of a stallion, stomping at the turf. A boot in the stirrups. "Is it Doctor Smith?" he wondered.

Burgess kept one hand clamped on Henry's mouth, and with the other he drew out his pistol. Henry squirmed under the weight of Burgess's body. It was useless: Burgess pressed the muzzle of his pistol hard against Henry's cheek and drew his lips back in a threatening snarl.

Smith walked his horse slowly around the side of the cottage.

A bird flapped into the air. Henry saw Smith climb from his horse, and approach the cottage.

Burgess stiffened. "Kelly's in there!" he muttered, and raised his pistol.

A creak as the back door opened. Smith entered. Then a swish as the front door opened, and the rush of feet, followed by a scraping and bumping noise as if some large object was being dragged across the ground towards them.

There was a crackle and snap of vegetation and Kelly crashed headlong into the ferns next to Burgess and Henry. He hauled another shape into the ferns alongside him, then collapsed on his back, gasping from exertion.

Henry's eyes popped: the bundle that Kelly had just dumped in the ferns was his mother Victoria. Her hands were bound with rope and a cloth pulled tight across her mouth.

Neither of them could say a word, but their eyes met in a mixture of fear and relief.

"Good man, Kelly!" chuckled Burgess. He shook his head in disbelief. "Well done!"

Burgess ducked low as Smith emerged from the cottage. "Where are you?" the doctor shouted.

Crack! Doctor Smith fired a shot from his revolver. A bullet smashed through the ferns and whistled past the hidden outlaws. Kelly whimpered and began shaking. Burgess signalled him to stay low. He half-expected the nervous Kelly to burst from his hiding place like a game bird flushed out by hunters.

Burgess held his grip on Henry's mouth, and Henry tried to use his eyes to signal to his mother: "It's all right. We'll be all right."

Then ... the whinny of a horse ... and Smith galloped away.

Burgess waited until the hoofbeats had faded, then released his grip. Henry gulped some air: "Mother! Are you all right?"

She nodded, prompting Kelly to push her head into the ferns.

"Holy Mother," he whined. "That man wants to kill us!"

Burgess snorted. "I've killed plenty like 'im."

TWENTY-EIGHT
SULLIVAN RETURNS

Burgess hauled Henry to his feet and told his accomplice, "Kelly, take 'er back in the 'ouse. We need to git goin'."

Kelly tugged on the ropes to make Henry's mother stand, and prodded her towards the cottage. Without warning, she turned and head butted him so hard he was sent sprawling.

Burgess roared with laughter. "Attaboy, Kelly!"

Kelly, cussing, scrambled to his feet and grabbed the ropes around his captive's hands. He jerked them hard, and she cried out through the gag.

"Mother!" Henry could see her wrists were bleeding where the ropes had cut into them.

"Kelly, 'old onto her!" ordered Burgess. "Tie 'er up nice 'n' tight now."

Kelly half carried, half dragged Henry's mother back towards the cottage. Henry began to follow her, but Burgess pushed his arm so far up his back that he cried out in pain.

"Move!" snapped Burgess. He held Henry's arm behind his back and frogmarched him through the trees. Henry looked back to see his mother being dragged into the cottage.

Burgess pushed his way through the undergrowth. They marched some hundred yards before they reached a nest the gang had created by trampling down the bracken. Burgess jabbed an elbow into Henry's ribs. "We been forced to 'ide here like rats, 'cos of that doctor o' yours snoopin' around."

"Why don't you leave then, before he finds you," blurted Henry.

Burgess raised his fist, then changed his mind. "There'll be gentlemen 'ere soon wiv gold," he said.

"It's not right!" Henry protested.

Burgess shook his head. "You're such a self-right-eous li'l prig, 'Enry! It's 'ard to believe you're me own son."

"I'm not your son," Henry muttered.

Kelly joined them with the physician's rifle, took out a knife, and began to carve his name into the butt.

Henry was horrified. "Stop it! That's the doctor's!"

"Ooh, that's the doctor's!" Kelly mimicked him, and continued carving.

Henry slumped back in the heather. "How has this happened?" he thought. The gang had taken his mother hostage, they had his horse and the physician's rifle, and he was a prisoner too. Could it be any worse?

THUMP! A boot struck his chest.

"Aieeeee!" Henry yelped in pain. He recognized the boots: Sullivan was back.

"I shoulda burked ya before!" snarled the big man.

"Lay off, Sullivan," Burgess intervened. "What news?"

But Sullivan didn't pay Burgess any attention. "This slimy little toad is interferin' with our plans!" He clamped a big hand on Henry's throat. Henry gurgled. "I might just give 'im his ticket o' leave, right now," said Sullivan, tightening his grip.

Henry was bug-eyed. He flung his arms and kicked his legs, but Sullivan was far too strong.

"Get yer 'ands off 'im, knucklehead!" Burgess yelled at Sullivan. He tried to pry Sullivan's hands away, but he could not.

Henry was red in the face and desperate for breath.

"Dammit, Sullivan – he's me son!"

"What?" Sullivan relaxed his grip but kept his knee on Henry.

Henry gulped in air.

"Watcha mean, he's yer son?" demanded Sullivan.

Burgess put away his pistol. "Me son. God's troof. I bin lookin' for 'im for years."

Sullivan let go of Henry and slammed his hands on Burgess's shoulders. "You goin' soft, Burgess?"

Burgess struggled to get free. "Let go, ya fool!"

Henry was wide-eyed as he watched the two accomplices fight.

"Cool it, Sullivan!" yelled Burgess. "We got to work togevva."

For a moment it looked as though Sullivan would strike his mate. Then he pulled back and let go.

"This kid'll turn you in, son or no son," he warned.

"No good'll come from snuffin' 'im," retorted Burgess.

"Ye'll regret this," said Sullivan. "Mark me words." He looked at Henry through narrowed eyes. "He knows too much."

The big man smirked. "Anyway – you ain't gonna talk, are ya, sonny?" He took something from his pocket.

Henry gasped. "Miriama!"

The object Sullivan dangled in front of him was a scarf.

Miriama's scarf.

TWENTY-NINE
A SECOND HOSTAGE

HENRY LOOKED WITH HORROR AT MIRIAMA'S SCARF AS Sullivan waved it in his face. Sullivan sneered.

"Turns out the doctor's little sidekick is actually a bird."

Burgess responded sternly.

"We don't harm womenfolk, remember?"

Henry believed him. He'd heard Burgess say this before. "We all have muvvas and sisters of our own."

But Sullivan was dismissive. "Back off, Burgess. No harm in a bit o' fun."

He dangled Miriama's scarf in front of Henry again. "Ooh, she's a feisty wee tart!" he taunted.

With dismay Henry saw fresh blood on Sullivan's shirt, and a scratch on his cheek. He couldn't bear to think Miriama had been harmed – or even killed.

"What've you done to her?"

"Nothing – yet," Sullivan grinned. "Savin' her for later."

"Where is she?" Henry yelled.

"Shuddup!"

Sullivan pushed him, this time with Smith's doctor's bag.

"She's safe, as long as you're a good wee boy."

Henry struggled to his knees. He looked past Sullivan – and saw Miriama lying unconscious on the ground, hands tied behind her.

"Miriama!" he cried out.

Burgess turned to Sullivan.

"What the 'ell did ya bring 'er for?"

"To make sure he behaves himself."

"We've already got his muvva."

Sullivan smirked. "Quit complainin', yer majesty."

He slung Miriama over his bony shoulder and marched to the cottage.

Henry appealed to Burgess.

"Don't let him hurt her!"

But Burgess was not sympathetic.

"You brung this on yerself, 'Enry." He yanked Henry to his feet.

At this moment Levy appeared, breathless. His smart clothes were spattered with mud.

"Comrades!" he called. "What gives?"

He saw Sullivan disappearing into the cottage with Miriama, and frowned at Henry, who was still red in the face.

"Too many witnesses!"

"Not for long," Kelly piped up, and slashed his finger across his throat.

Were they really going to kill them all? Henry wondered.

Burgess signalled to Levy.

"Spill the beans, bruvver."

"They'll be here presently. Three men, five packhorses."

Burgess rubbed his hands.

"It's on, lads! Look sharp, Kelly."

Sullivan returned with a leather thong, and secured Henry's hands tight behind his back. He put his bushy face next to Henry's ear and whispered:

"Got me eye on you, kid."

Henry shuddered.

The men had found a dark 'tunnel' through the dense undergrowth – perhaps one of the many short cuts hacked through the bushes by Māori war parties – and they wound their way through in single file. Levy was up front, followed by Sullivan. Kelly dawdled, humming, carrying Henry's rifle.

Burgess pushed Henry ahead of him through the scrub. Hands pulled behind his back, Henry concentrated on keeping his footing.

Suddenly Levy hissed, "Down!"

Everyone dropped. Henry gasped as Burgess tugged his thongs to force him to his knees.

"Horseman," said Levy.

Henry peered through the scrub and was alarmed to see Doctor Smith on horseback some hundred paces away.

"It's 'im!" snarled Sullivan.

Doctor Smith stood tall in his stirrups, searching the undergrowth, and yelled:

"Come out, you murderer!"

Smith raised one of his pearl-handled pistols and fired.

CRACK!

A bullet rocketed – WOOSH – through the leaves close to Kelly.

Kelly whimpered, and crouched lower. "Why me?"

Henry wondered if he should call out. But Sullivan read his thoughts, and clamped a grimy hand across his mouth.

They huddled behind the bushes: Levy, Kelly and Burgess and Sullivan, both holding Henry down. After a time Burgess peered out.

"Gawn," he announced.

"Looks like he's off to Canvas Town," said Levy.

Sullivan removed his hand, allowing Henry to gulp in air. He lay back on the ground, chest heaving. He didn't see Smith ride off. But Sullivan watched keenly.

"That'll keep him out of the way while we attend to business," he said. He continued to watch Smith as he rode into the distance.

Burgess looked at him quizzically. Sullivan glared back. "What?"

"D'you know that geezer, Sullivan?"

"What you sayin'?"

"Well," said Burgess, "yer look like ya seen a ghost."

Sullivan merely grunted. He cracked his knuckles and followed Levy. Burgess looked at Smith's receding figure too, frowning, as if trying to recall something.

THIRTY
MURDERERS' ROCK

THE PARTY EMERGED FROM THE TRACK AND THERE BEFORE them was the Maungatapu rock.

"A beautiful spot for a pinch of mischief!" cried Burgess.

Our young hero had been intrigued when Doctor Smith remarked that it would be an ideal place for an ambush. And now, here was the common outlaw Richard Burgess expressing the same sentiment.

"A bee-autiful spot," Burgess repeated. He looked back and forth, up and down the track, imagining how he and his gang might waylay a party of wealthy travellers. Tall trees and scrub lined one side of the road, and the other side dropped away to a steep gully. The track was barely wide enough for a pair of horses to pass, and it was pitted with rocks and indentations.

"A bee-autiful spot!" Burgess dragged Henry behind the rock and ordered him to sit. With the arrogance and certainty of a man accustomed to being obeyed, he lectured Henry to observe him and his associates as they set the trap.

"Watch an' learn, son," he said. "Watch an' learn."

As Burgess moved away, his odious companion Sullivan moved next to Henry. He grabbed Henry by the hair and forced his head back, then stuffed Miriama's scarf in the young man's mouth, holding it tight in place with his own soiled neckerchief. Henry gagged, and forced himself to calm his breathing, lest he choke to death.

"That'll learn ya," Sullivan rumbled.

Sullivan placed Dr Smith's medical bag in front of him, and grunted as he examined its contents. The stethoscope was only of momentary interest, for the man did not know what it was. But he recognized a bottle of laudanum and sniffed it. "Happy times!" He secreted the bottle in his jacket pocket and smirked at Henry.

What he did not realise was that our young hero was already acting out a plan of escape. He had located, behind him, a sharp-edged rock against which he could rub his leather bonds, and even as Sullivan was mocking his distress he was working to break free.

And here, my dear reader, we might credit this humble author's book *"Incident in Death Valley"*, in which we recounted how a resourceful cowhand freed himself by working his rope ties against a rock. Henry recalled this chapter and performed the same action, and was pleased to learn how quickly the jagged edge of a rock can cut into leather.

Burgess and Sullivan worked together to clear the undergrowth to make a path off the main track, no doubt with a dastardly plan in mind. Sullivan was a reluctant helpmate, and Henry was reminded that these two villains, although members of the same gang, held no love for each other.

A cry rang out: "Someone coming!"

It was Levy, the lookout, who had seen an old man approaching their position. The gang took cover as Jamie Battle shuffled towards them.

I do not propose to dwell on the ugly incident which followed. Much has been written about the brutal manner in which Sullivan, claiming the old flax-cutter was concealing gold upon his person, sent the poor fellow to meet his Maker. "Murder most foul!" the old man cried, but Sullivan showed him no more mercy than a wolf gives a rabbit.

We know that Sullivan escaped the gallows for

other murders, but it was this slaying of Jamie Battle for which he was sent to prison and widely loathed.

Let us move quickly to the events that followed. For even as Sullivan dealt the death blow, Henry's leather bonds gave way. He leapt to his feet and took hold of the doctor's medical bag. Kelly was taken by surprise and reached for the rifle, but Henry swung the bag at him with all his strength, and sent the gun flying. As Kelly scrabbled to retrieve the rifle, Henry turned and ran like a hare pursued by hounds.

Now at last he was able to pull down Sullivan's neckerchief and take Miriama's scarf from his mouth. He gulped in fresh air as he galloped down the track and into the bushes.

But this was not to be the clean getaway he had wanted, for Sullivan appeared on the track behind him and bellowed "Come back, you little toad!"

Sullivan's cry was followed quickly by another from Levy the lookout. "They're coming!" he called, pointing to the distant figures of several businessmen with their loaded packhorses. "The diggers are here!"

This was the party they planned to rob, and Henry hoped that the arrival of gold-bearing travellers would distract Sullivan from his own situation. But it was not to be. Both Sullivan and Kelly set off in pursuit of our young hero.

Henry came to clear ground, and with his youth and heightened state of excitement it seemed he would quickly shake off his pursuers. But in an instant this hope vanished.

Henry came to an abrupt halt: he realised he was at the very brink of a ravine, and he peered aghast at the rock-strewn creek far below.

"I am done!" he said.

THIRTY-ONE
WAITING TO DIE

Henry turned to face his pursuers, hoping they might simply take him captive again. But Sullivan, having being persuaded twice by Burgess to spare the young man's life, was not to be denied again. He raised his pistol and lined up his target.

Henry involuntarily lifted the doctor's bag in front of his body, even as he heard the *crack* of Sullivan's pistol.

The bullet hit the bag hard, and although the thick leather stopped its travel, the force of the deadly metal knocked Henry off his feet. He was hurled backwards, tumbling over and over, crashing down the cliff face towards the creek. The bag had saved him, and now the wiry bushes broke his momentum. Still, the crunch with which he finally hit the creek was enough to wind him.

He lay in the shallows, scratched and bruised, gasping like a beached fish, aware that someone's blood was billowing into a thin cloud in the water around his body. As his mind cleared, he realised he was still holding Sullivan's neckerchief in his hand. He released it and watched it drift away with the current.

He heard Kelly call out "Hey!"

The way Henry had landed, his face was turned away from the cliff and the man at the top, and he was not inclined to turn around to greet him. He lay as still as the rocks around him, confident that if he did not move a muscle he would be presumed dead.

"He looks dead," said Kelly, not wishing to follow Henry down the cliff to make sure. But Sullivan wanted certainty.

"Finish him awf," he told Kelly, "and get the bag."

"Why me?" grizzled Kelly. But he began to ease himself down the cliff.

Our young hero lay motionless, his bleeding head causing him pain, but he was determined not to move. He heard Kelly cussing as he clawed his way down the slope. Sullivan had gone, off to make a bloody rendezvous with the gold-carrying travellers.

Kelly was a reluctant adventurer, keen to protect his expensive new waistcoat, and after slipping and sliding halfway down the cliff face, any enthusiasm vanished when his precious waistcoat caught on a branch.

"Oh, Lordy! That's done it!"

Henry waited for Kelly's next move. In the distance he heard a man's desperate cry, and knew that there were other innocent men in an equal if not worse predicament than he.

"Hey, you!" Kelly yelled again. He threw a lump of clay, and Henry gasped as it hit his head.

The nearby *crack* of a rifle seemed to agitate Kelly even more. He picked up a rock which was barely small enough to fit into his palm, and hurled it.

Had the rock struck Henry on the head it would have been the end of him, and his story would have progressed no further. But the missile instead found Henry's leg.

Now Henry had experienced pain many times. The worst was when he swung a mallet intended to drive a nail into the fence but instead hit his thumb. The second worst was when Duke kicked him in the chest and broke two ribs. On both occasions Henry had experienced excruciating pain that brought him to tears. But these were nothing compared to the red hot arrows which shot through his leg as Kelly's rock hit him.

He screamed without making a sound. It was testament to his courage and determination that, even though he knew his leg must be broken, he did not writhe or struggle. And he knew, even through his agony, that Kelly would now turn away in the certain knowledge that his quarry was dead.

He lay there in the creek, one hand gripping Miriama's scarf, feigning death. He counted to ten. He counted to a hundred. He took deep breaths in an effort to subdue the pain that ran up and down his leg. He counted to a hundred again.

Then came another scream from near the track, where Burgess and his gang were carrying out their heinous crimes. Henry turned his head slowly, cautiously, to gain a view of the cliff face. Kelly was nowhere to be seen. He must surely have returned to join his mates to help complete their bloody business.

Henry raised his torso, ignoring the pain, and began to drag himself through the water to the far bank. But as he moved his leg across the rocks, the pain was intolerable. He allowed himself a cry. A loud, piteous cry. And Kelly heard it. He appeared halfway up the cliff, and let loose the bellow of an enraged bull before slipping and crashing back down the slope, wielding the physician's rifle and ignoring the branches that clawed at his waistcoat.

Henry moved fast. By some miracle he became a man whose legs were in fine form. He took hold of the doctor's bag and scrambled onto the far bank. Kelly reached the creek and fell into it, striking his shoulder on the rocks. He turned as he heard a man's pleading voice in the distance, and when he looked back Henry had disappeared into the undergrowth.

Kelly plunged into the dark bushes after him, and was promptly ambushed by a furious wildcat who fell upon him and sent him flying. Henry used all his flagging strength to push Kelly into the creek, and took possession of the bag again before burrowing back into the undergrowth. The pain in his leg was beyond any pain he had ever endured, but to stop now would be to face execution. In a haze of pain and desperation he forced aside the saplings and vines that clung to him and made good progress before dropping onto the leafy forest floor to rest.

"Mother of God!" Kelly spluttered. He knew he would face the wrath of his comrade in crime Sullivan when he confessed he had lost both their runaway captive and the doctor's bag, but he also knew it would be futile trying to follow the young man into the dense undergrowth. He cussed and sloshed back across the creek to climb out of the ravine and rejoin his gang.

THIRTY-TWO
THE RIFLE AGAIN

KELLY FOUND HIS MATES IN A CLEARING IN THE FOREST, picking over the spoils from their crimes. He did not need to ask what fate had befallen the ambushed travellers: there was a saddlebag resting at Sullivan's feet and he and Levy were sorting through documents and letters for anything that could be converted into cash.

Sullivan looked up as Kelly joined them. "Dunnit?" he asked.

Kelly nodded. Sullivan had forgotten for the moment that Kelly should have been carrying the doctor's bag, and seemed to accept his assurance that Henry had been successfully dispatched. Kelly propped the rifle against a tree stump and looked around for a distraction. He did not have long to wait, for Burgess handed him a shovel and told him:

"Get busy, Kelly, and dig a respectable grave."

"Why me?" Kelly grumbled. He removed his precious waistcoat and hung it on a branch, moaning as he fingered the rips and holes caused by the scrubby bushes in the ravine.

He jabbed the shovel into the ground, and found it was a hard clay that would require much sweat before he could call it a burial plot. As was his custom, he began complaining aloud.

"I don't know why ..." he said. "The dirtiest, smelliest, toughest, most harrowing, ignominious, unnecessary..."

Sullivan called out: "Stop whining, Kelly." He held up a handful of bank notes retrieved from the saddlebag. "You're gonna be rich enough to buy the prettiest waistcoat in town."

They had lit a fire, and Sullivan and Levy began burning documents from the bag which had no value to them.

"These crafty businessmen have not died in vain," Sullivan laughed. "They have bequeathed us a fine treasure trove."

"Enough for our tickets to Australia?"

"Enough for some fine clothes too, and enough rum to stop your shaking, Kelly."

Kelly looked down at his hands, and clenched the

shovel tighter to stop them trembling.

He was about to complain when Burgess reappeared from the bushes. He was hauling the body of a man in a businessman's suit.

"You done, Kelly?" asked Burgess.

Kelly scooped up a pile of dirt. "I'm stuffed," he moaned.

"Lazy prick," said Sullivan.

Burgess dumped the body on the spot Kelly had marked out.

"Cover him with rocks," he ordered. Kelly muttered but went to find more rocks.

Now all this time our young hero, having regained some of his strength, had established the gang's whereabouts and was lying in the bushes at the edge of the clearing, awaiting an opportunity to recover the physician's rifle. Kelly and Burgess were now occupied with the grisly task of piling rocks onto the dead man, and Henry made his move.

He crawled forward to the edge of the clearing and reached out for the rifle.

It did not cause him much concern that he was in the presence of four felons who had just murdered four innocent gold miners and businessmen. Or that these desperadoes would most certainly add him to their list of victims if they caught him. All that mattered to him was to retrieve the physician's rifle. He would not rest if it remained in the hands of these evil men.

He took hold of the weapon and pulled it slowly towards him.

Henry would not rest if the physician's rifle
remained in the hands of these evil men

"By the time they find the bodies we'll be long gone," Burgess told his accomplices.

Henry slithered back through the mouldering

leaves, pulling the rifle alongside him, then half stood and staggered away, all time suppressing his own screams as his injury sent bolts of lightning up his leg.

He found a narrow path formed by the Māori warriors who sometimes traversed this area, and hurried along it. He stopped briefly to listen to the commotion back at the gang site.

"Me rifle!" cried Kelly. "It's gone!"

"Where was it?" demanded Sullivan.

"Just there. It's gone." Henry envisaged Kelly's panicked expression.

"Are you sure you didn't leave it back there?" asked Burgess.

"Kelly," said Sullivan menacingly, and Henry knew the big man would be standing over poor Kelly, his fist clenched. "Did you finish him awf?"

"The kid? Sure I did."

"You're a bloody liar, Kelly," barked Sullivan.

THUMP! This was the sound of Sullivan's fist against Kelly's chest, and the smaller man gasped as the air was forced from his lungs.

Henry took the rifle and continued his forced march through the bushes. He knew the gang would very shortly be in hot pursuit.

Sullivan rounded on Burgess.

"I warned you, Burgess. That kid'll be our undoing. I

don't care if he's your son or King Arthur – he's a traitor."

Burgess ignored him but yelled at Kelly:

"Kelly – go and make sure the women are still tied up."

"Why me?"

"Just go, Kelly," snapped Burgess.

Kelly grizzled but found a path and entered it.

Henry could hear Kelly stomping along the track, much faster than he could travel with his injured leg. His strength was ebbing as he hobbled on.

Finally he could go no further. He staggered off the path, burrowed into the ferns, and collapsed.

Through his pain he could hear Kelly approaching. He could not move further out of the way, and he could not even keep his eyes open. He slipped into unconsciousness.

Kelly marched right past him, cussing and muttering loudly.

And Henry dreamt.

He dreamt he was a lawman, astride a powerful stallion, being chased across the prairie by a horde of Red Indians. Arrows flew past him as he crouched low in the saddle. Occasionally he returned fire with his pearl-handled pistol, and was satisfied to see another Indian brave topple from his pony. But he knew they were gaining on him, and the safety of the fort was just a speck on the horizon. He was done for.

A horseman drew alongside him. It was Richard Burgess, bearded and terrifying. He raised his tomahawk above his head and swung it hard into Henry's leg. Henry screamed.

He awoke moaning, and clutching his leg.

The pain was unbearable. But he had to carry on. To reach his mother. To rescue Miriama.

How long had he been unconscious?

The forest was just as dark as before. No sunlight could penetrate the canopy of trees and ferns. Henry tried to stand, but he cried out in pain, and fell unconscious again.

THIRTY-THREE
SHOWDOWN AT PRITCHARD'S COTTAGE

NOT SO FAR AWAY, IN THE ABANDONED COTTAGE AT Pritchard's Glade, Henry's mother and his beloved Miriama had been diligently working to free themselves.

The younger woman pulled away the last of the strands of rope from her wrists, and began to loosen the knots that held Henry's mother.

But their joy was short-lived.

They heard a creak on the old floorboards and the highwayman Kelly stood at the door, pistol in hand.

His jacket was awry, boots muddied, and his bushy sideburns and moustache were moist from the dripping ferns he had pushed through.

"Good God!" he cried. "What are you doing?!"

He waved his pistol wildly.

"Lie down, both of you!"

Miriama obeyed, dropping to her knees with her arms around Henry's mother. Unseen by Kelly, she wrenched undone the last knot around her companion's wrists. They were now both free to spring into action, but the time was not right as Kelly marched up and down the small room in anger and indecision.

"Of all the thankless, needless, regrettable ... Why me? Why this poor Irishman whose only sin is to seek a free life under the stars ... Why me?"

He looked around, wide eyed, as if he expected his comrades to suddenly join him.

"Where are you, Burgess?"

The women stared in wonder as Kelly raved, and waited for their moment.

Kelly was undoubtedly capable of brutal and violent behaviour, and indeed he had served time in Australia for highway robbery, but he was not capable of making quick decisions. After his release from prison, he had teamed up with Richard Burgess and had been most content to follow his mate's orders.

He leant over the two women as they huddled on the floor and yelled at them.

"You don't know what my friends are capable of!"

At that moment, he was startled by the dull thud of wood striking wood. Henry had arrived, but in his exhausted state he had allowed his rifle to strike the door frame. Having lost the element of surprise, he had to act quickly.

Ignoring the pain that still electrified his body, he dropped the rifle and leapt at Kelly barehanded.

"Holy Mother!" the outlaw cried, and pulled at the trigger of his pistol.

With a sharp *crack* the bullet shattered the front window, and shards of glass spattered across the floor.

Henry gripped Kelly in an almighty bear hug, pinning the man's arms to his side, and the two of them tottered around the room in a kind of clumsy dance.

"Let me go!" the highwayman cried out. But Henry found the strength to maintain his hold. He was determined that his prisoner would remain so.

The two women were not slow in coming to Henry's assistance. Their limbs were aching from their hours of bondage, but they had the passion and strength of mountain lionesses defending their cubs.

Miriama had found an old frying pan and directed it with great effect at Kelly's gun hand. *Whack!* He dropped the pistol and roared in pain. But his female avengers were far from finished: Henry's mother swung a heavy cooking pot and brought it down on the Irishman's skull. *Thunk!*

Kelly became a dead weight. Henry released his hold and let the intruder crumple to the floor.

"Miriama! Mother!" he cried. His legs finally gave way beneath him and he fell to the floor, his eyes rolling and hands twitching.

Miriama knelt beside him, nursing his head, as his mother picked up Kelly's pistol. The man groaned and got to his knees, swaying and clutching his head. He felt the blood trickling down his forehead and gave his assailants a startled look.

"Mother of God! You've murdered me!"

Despite the desperate situation and the recent turn of events, Victoria Appleton could not control her laughter.

"You despicable creature!"

She gave Kelly a shove which sent him staggering out the door. He was in no doubt that the best course of action was to retreat into the bushes, and this is what he did.

Victoria turned her attention to her injured son. His face was as pale as the snow she had not seen for many years, and his temperature was raging.

"Hurry, hurry!" Henry called out.

The women looked at each in wonder. They were not to know that Henry was back on the prairie, still in flight from the Indians who were close behind him. He dug his boots into Duke's side and pleaded for the stallion to increase his speed. The Indians were surrounding him. There was Kelly, waving his pistol, throwing rocks, raving. And Burgess, with the body of a dead businessman draped across his saddle. Now Sullivan joined them, and suddenly they were all on the ground and the big man was pounding his leg with his fists.

And through it all came the sweet voice of an angel.

"Be strong, Henry," said the voice. "I love you."

And despite the confusion of his dream, and the pain pulsing through his body, Henry knew the angel was Miriama.

Everything would work out.

THIRTY-FOUR
SEARCH PARTY

An American farmer would struggle to adequately describe to a citizen of New Zealand the awesome power of a dust storm in Kansas or Oklahoma. But likewise, that same farmer would have difficulty in contemplating a winter rainstorm in New Zealand. The opening of the heavens, and the relentless hammering of heavy raindrops on the earth ... followed by the sudden roar of streams cascading down the mountains, sweeping away trees and rocks.

Thus it was on Friday, June the 29th, 1866, as dozens of citizens scoured the bleak mountainside above Nelson township for any sign of the missing travellers from Canvas Town.

A storm had flooded the creek and lashed the trees and bushes in the past few days, and rain still hammered the undergrowth, bending ferns under its weight.

Here we find our young hero Henry Appleton huddled under an oilskin, his walking stick resting at his side, and his injured leg stretched out straight before him. He peers into the mist, scribbling in his sketch book as rain-soaked police, shopkeepers, cabinet makers and farm hands search the mountainside.

Richard Burgess had been confident it would be several days before the bodies of the murdered men were found, thus giving the gang time to catch a ship to another part of the country, and then on to Australia. But he was wrong.

The gold miners and businessmen from Canvas Town had been reported missing the very next day ... and a search party of volunteers was formed to scour the hills.

The searchers' spirits had been lifted by the discovery of several items which they presumed the Burgess gang had abandoned: a shovel which probably belonged to the hapless flax-cutter, a blood-spotted Crimean shirt, and a loaded double-barrelled shotgun.

They had also found the body of Old Farmer, the packhorse which belonged to one of the missing men. The horse had been shot dead.

By now everyone knew, or at least suspected, that the missing men had been murdered.

There were around 90 searchers in the hills. Some of them formed a human chain, spaced a yard apart, looking for clues. Perhaps they were spurred on by talk of a reward for the discovery of the missing men's bodies. But there was also a communal sense of horror and indignation that the peace of this respectable township had been shattered.

Among the searchers were Doctor Zephaniah Smith and Sergeant John Nash, both on horseback, water dripping from their hats.

Henry's young friend Miriama was there too, dressed in men's clothes, and wrapped in an oilskin coat so oversized that it dragged in the mud.

No newspaperman worth his salt would miss this opportunity to be a part of history, and so it was that I found myself on the hillside that miserable morning. For a while I watched Henry sketching the scene and then greeted him.

"Henry!"

My voice startled Henry. He turned to see my imposing figure, wearing a cowboy hat and oilskin coat as though I had stepped straight out of one of my Western novels.

"Mister Slick!"

I looked around at the searchers dotted over the hillside.

"Just like the Wild West, huh?"

"Yes, but it doesn't seem romantic in any way."

"Word is, Henry – you're a hero."

Henry shook his head.

"No, no."

"Well ..." I said, "ya bin kidnapped and shot, broke ya leg, and helped catch a bunch o' vermin. Sure sounds like a hero to me."

"I'm just glad to be alive," mumbled Henry.

I slapped him on the back.

"Good on ya, kid. You bin writing your own story. Just like I told ya."

Then, up in the bush-clad slopes, a bugle sounded, and men came running.

A body had been found.

Searchers converged on the spot, and Henry and I joined them. It was not long before there were more grisly discoveries.

Henry's pencil recorded it all: the ugly handiwork of Richard Burgess, Joseph Sullivan, Thomas Kelly, and Philip Levy – described by Burgess as his band of 'merry men'. "There's nothing merry about what they've done," Henry thought.

Henry sketched men lifting rocks to uncover the

battered body of gold miner James De Pontius of New York. He was lying face down, his hat next to his head. Henry shuddered as he remembered watching Kelly and Burgess piling rocks on the dead man.

He sketched a police constable as he discovered the body of Felix Mathieu, the Frenchman who used to run the Café de Paris pub at Deep Creek. He was lying on his back, mouth open.

He sketched John Kempthorne, crumpled, shot through the head.

And James Dudley, face to the ground, a handkerchief around his neck. Strangled.

The bodies were deep in the bush, and the gang had not bothered to bury them. They had piled rocks on De Pontius's body and only thrown branches across the others.

Henry stopped sketching and looked away, pondering how he had once been tempted by the offer of joining Burgess's gang.

He watched a procession of men carrying bodies down the mountain track through the mist and rain. The bodies were cradled in canvas hammocks, slung on poles. All victims of Burgess's merry men.

Henry's tears mingled with the rain as he listened to the sloshing of the searchers' boots on the rain-soaked mountain path, and the creak of the poles as they strained under the weight of the bodies.

On the outskirts of town the men passed an ensemble of half a dozen musicians – violins, cello, viola – who were accompanying local butcher Billy Hargreaves as he sang *Messe de requiem*.

At the head of the procession was Sergeant Major Robert Shallcrass, in charge of the police in the district.

When they reached the road, they laid the bodies on horse-drawn drays and carted them to a makeshift morgue in the Nelson Fire Brigade engine house.

Henry stood in the crowd as the volunteers marched up Trafalgar Street to the Trafalgar Hotel to report to the search committee. The marchers were sombre, but mighty satisfied their exhausting days in the bush had resulted in the discovery of the missing men's bodies. Along the way they were cheered by crowds of locals.

Next day, the *Nelson Express* informed anyone who had not heard the news:

BODIES OF MISSING MEN FOUND
ON MAUNGATAPU MOUNTAIN.

What happened next was baffling.

THIRTY-FIVE
ARRESTS

RICHARD BURGESS AND HIS THREE CRONIES, WITH BLOOD ON their hands and stolen coins in their pockets, skulked into Nelson promising each other they would lay low until they could catch a ride on a steamer. But they proceeded to make themselves conspicuous by going shopping, drinking in bars, wandering around town and striking up conversations with locals.

Their rough attire, shifty demeanour and ready money made them obvious suspects when townsfolk learnt that several travellers had gone missing on their way from Canvas Town to Nelson. Burgess and his crew were arrested in quick time.

The ugly events of the past few days were still fresh in Henry's mind: his bullying at the hands of Sullivan;

the pain as Kelly's rock struck his leg; the screams of the murdered men in the hills. He was left with a physical dread of the gang, especially after seeing the bodies of their victims in the hills. Nevertheless, he was determined that he would put aside his fear and sketch the arrests of the villains.

And so it was that he found himself leaning against the side of a wooden building with his artist's sketchbook in hand.

Keeping well out of the way, he completed a sketch of Richard Burgess – perhaps his father? – being arrested by Constable Bartholomew Murphy as he walked along Bridge Street.

And, sketchbook in hand, he went with the police to the Wakatū Hotel and watched as they arrested Levy, who was sipping a beer and did not put up a struggle. Later, Henry was with the police when they stopped Kelly as he came out of the dining room of the Lord Nelson Hotel. Loudmouthed Kelly, the man who had sniggered as he carved his name into the physician's rifle, was now a whimpering prisoner.

And Henry watched as constables entered the Mitre Hotel and found Sullivan sitting with a glass of wine. This time, Henry stood in the background with his sketchbook. He had no desire to confront this violent man.

He stepped back into the shadows as they brought Sullivan out in handcuffs. The big man, with his mouth a crack in the rock of his face, had his fists clenched tight.

"He still gives me the shivers," Henry thought.

THIRTY-SIX
FAREWELLS

HENRY APPLETON WAS THE TALK OF THE TOWN ONCE NEWS OF his adventures began to fill the columns of Nelson's newspapers. Not only did those papers recount his terrifying ordeal at the hands of the Burgess gang, and his heroic rescue of his mother and Miriama, but they discovered in their archives their earlier stories about the 10-year-old Henry who had helped to catch the Nelson bank robbers.

The newspapers published these stories again, and Henry was soon dubbed the town's 'Boy Hero', a name which to his embarrassment was used by all and sundry at every public event he attended.

Richard Burgess, on the other hand, was dubbed by the *Gazette* as "The most hated man in the country –

and for good reason. Nelson is a place of industrious and honest citizens."

These 'honest citizens' were horrified by details of the Maungatapu murders. But they were also fascinated by the evil in their midst. To feed the public's hunger for detail, newspaper reporters interviewed any witness who claimed to have seen the murderous gang on their march up the South Island, and artists were commissioned to draw maps and sketches of the gang's travels. Groups of giggling young people trekked up into the hills to visit what was now referred to as Murderers' Rock.

It became known that Burgess had been cruelly mistreated by prison guards in Australia, but this did not excuse his own evil deeds. Some people in town claimed the gang had killed twenty or thirty men during their time in New Zealand.

But Burgess did not kill Doctor Smith's wife. This news, my friends, came as a considerable surprise and shock to the good doctor. Burgess had confessed to other killings, but he insisted he was innocent of the murder of Dr Smith's wife – and it was the doctor's own finger-printing gear that proved him right.

With the permission of the prison authorities, Smith brought his equipment into the prison one day and took a print of Burgess's thumb to compare it with the thumb print of the man who murdered Alicia Smith. And the prints did not match.

"This is not the man who murdered my wife," the doctor pronounced, his voice shaky.

Burgess was gleeful. "I told ya, I never done 'arm no lady!" he crowed.

The doctor was stunned. He had hunted Burgess for the best part of two years, certain that he was the killer. Now he knew he had been pursuing the wrong man. He packed up his gear and left the prison in despair.

Clearly, Dr Smith could have continued his search for his wife's killer, and most people expected he would. Indeed, Burgess immediately offered him the name of a prime suspect – his associate Sullivan.

But the doctor was exhausted, and quite possibly he was aware that his obsession for revenge was eating away at his own body and soul.

"I desperately want to see justice done," he told Henry outside the prison. "But the sergeant has said he is certain the Burgess gang will all be found guilty and hanged. So if Sullivan is my wife's murderer, he will pay with his life anyway."

Henry nodded. He was pleased at the doctor's decision to abandon his quest, recalling how shocked he was when the doctor declared that he was going to execute the killer himself.

"The Chinese have a proverb," continued the doctor. "Before embarking on a journey of revenge, prepare two graves."

Henry smiled. Miriama had quoted the same proverb.

"And I know it to be true," said the doctor in a shaky voice. "My search for the killer is destroying me, Henry."

He laid a hand on Henry's shoulder, and the young man realised the doctor was not comforting him but supporting himself. His whole body was trembling.

"For my own wellbeing, I must stop."

He took his hand off Henry's shoulder and held it out to shake Henry's hand.

"Goodbye Henry. I'm going back to Australia."

"What about the trial?" Henry asked.

"I cannot sit in court and listen to those weasels trying to justify what they've done."

Henry was hardly aware of Smith shaking his hand. He struggled for words.

"You're a good man, Henry," said Smith. "You'll make a fine doctor."

Henry looked at Smith blankly.

"I will send you money to pay for your training, Henry. To become a physician. Like I used to be."

"Used to be?"

Smith smiled. "Humanity needs people like you,

Henry. People with compassion. God knows, I no longer have any."

He turned to go.

"Wait!" Henry cried out. He scrabbled in his pocket and pulled out his pocket knife. He thrust it into Smith's hand.

"Please take this, sir."

Smith read the words inscribed on the handle.

"It says *'Henry Appleton, from your'* – Your father gave you this?"

Henry nodded. This was the very knife which William Appleton had presented to Henry only a year ago. Not for a birthday, nor for Christmas, but "as an expression of my love for you, my son." The gift had quite taken young Henry by surprise, for his adoptive father although compassionate had seldom shown Henry any personal affection. Looking back, Henry suspected that his father must already have been thinking of heading off to the goldfields, and knew there was a chance he might never return.

"You are a fine young man, Henry, and I am proud of you." These were William Appleton's last words to Henry, which he recalled with clarity and sadness.

Thus it was not without a pang of remorse that Henry handed the knife to Doctor Zephaniah Smith.

The doctor sighed deeply.

"Thank you Henry. This means the world."

The very next day Dr Zephaniah Smith took the boat back to Australia, and Miriama with him, as she had promised to continue acting as his assistant for another year.

Henry pined for his missing friends and struggled to lead a normal life.

Spring arrived, but it did not bring a fresh start or fresh hope for Henry. Although his injured leg was healing, he had been told he would always need to use a walking stick. The stick would be an everlasting reminder of his ordeal at the hands of the Burgess gang.

THIRTY-SEVEN
BURGESS'S FATE

HENRY AND MOST OF THE TOWN ATTENDED THE TRIAL OF THE
Maungatapu Murderers which began on September the
12th, 1866. Much has been written about it and I do not
propose to add more words, for the intention of this
modest novel is to celebrate the heroic deeds of Henry
Appleton.

Richard Burgess was sentenced to hang, along with
Thomas Kelly and Philip Levy. Sullivan, having turned
Queen's Evidence, was not put on trial for the murders
of the four travellers from Canvas Town, claiming he
was simply a lookout. But the very next day he was tried
and convicted for another crime – the murder of the old
flax-cutter Jamie Battle – and given a lengthy prison
term.

The hanging of the convicted murderers took place on Friday, October the 5th, 1866. Let us not dwell too long on this miserable event. This writer has been the reluctant witness to many hangings, all of them ugly affairs where no one is redeemed and nothing good is achieved, whether they occurred in the bitter cold of Alaska, or in the merciless heat of Mexico, or in the grey smog of a nameless city, or – as in this case – on a sunny morning in the prison yard of Nelson township.

The three condemned men, all having been found guilty of the Maungatapu Murders, were brought out into the prison yard and allowed to mingle with the police and prison officers and others who were there to act as official 'witnesses' to the execution.

Both Levy and Kelly continued to proclaim their innocence as they faced the gallows, and Kelly screamed as he was dragged to the rope. But Burgess calmly told everyone in a loud and clear voice: "I die, and I deserve my fate."

Thus ended a dark chapter in the history of Nelson township and in the life of Henry Appleton. In the course of a few harrowing months, this boy had become a man, and – as is well known now – he went on to become a doctor and marry Miriama.

Our story of Henry Appleton, Boy Hero might well

end here, but this writer must – somewhat reluctantly – add one final chapter. It relates to an incident which occurred in town on the very same day as the hangings, and it must be recorded because it goes to reinforce Henry's reputation as a true hero.

THIRTY-EIGHT
A NARROW ESCAPE

IT HAPPENED LIKE THIS.

On the afternoon of October the 5th, 1866 I, the novelist Johnny Slick, having witnessed the hangings of the Maungatapu Murderers, was in sore need of peace and quiet. To clear from my mind the ghastly images of three human beings swinging at the end of a rope.

I took a stroll down to the end of Bridge Street to admire the famous Eel Pond. It began to rain, a sudden Spring shower, so I wrapped my oilskin coat around me, pulled my hat low, and began to slosh back through the mud to the road.

I was surprised to see Henry Appleton and Sergeant Nash emerge from a nearby house, and I accosted Henry as to the reason for this visit. Henry confided that he had been to call on the family of one of the men who had been murdered by the Burgess gang, to give them the gold that had been recovered and was rightfully theirs.

Henry confessed that, to his shame, he had for a while considered keeping some of the gold for himself.

As a man more familiar with the disreputable behaviour of Western gunslingers, I was able to console Henry and applaud his honesty. But even as I began to speak along these lines, there was a great hullabaloo further down the road. Men were shouting, a dog was barking, and there was the ominous thunder of pounding hoofbeats.

I looked up in alarm and saw a 600 pound bullock charging directly towards me. A farmer was in hot pursuit of the animal, waving his staff and yelling obscenities.

"Watch out!" the farmer shouted.

Consider the scene, and this intrepid writer's predicament. The bullock is headed straight towards me, tossing its horns in readiness to impale any human in its way. I can see the froth in the beast's mouth, the crazed rolling of its eyes, and the powerful muscles on its flank.

In this terrifying moment, dear readers, the world stands still.

I am transfixed. I cannot decide whether to step to

my right or my left. So I do neither, and wait to be trampled into the dirt by this runaway locomotive.

"Watch out!" the farmer yells again.

The dog barks again. A woman screams. I hear nothing but the thundering of hooves.

Suddenly, miraculously, Johnny Slick is
propelled into the air, out of the path of the
great bullock

I do not see Henry charge at me. All I know is that suddenly, miraculously, I am propelled into the air, out of the path of the great bullock.

Yours truly, Johnny Slick, a man of significant proportions himself, his coat billowing and hat spinning, hurtles off the side of the road and down the bank towards the eel pond.

Henry follows, tumbling head over heels in the mud.

We come to rest only feet from the murky waters of the pond. I gather my breath and watch with considerable relief as the bullock gallops past me and continues off down the road, with the dog yapping at its hooves.

The farmer pauses, puffing.

"Well done, lad!" he grins at Henry. "Never seen a kid lift a grown man off his feet before!"

He turns to me. "You're a lucky gentleman, sir, for sure. Reckon you owe the lad a pint." Then he resumes his pursuit of the bullock.

Henry Appleton and I look at each other in silence. Two great adventurers and writers, sprawled side by side in the mud, panting from exertion and excitement.

Our clothes have a liberal covering of slimy mud. Our hats lie forlornly on the roadside, along with Henry's walking stick.

I spit out mud and grass, wipe my beard, and gasp: "In all ma days ... !"

I knew at that moment that I owed my life to the brave actions of Nelson's quick-witted boy hero, Henry Appleton himself. What a privilege! What a story!

A great sound began to rumble from my belly, and I bellowed with laughter until my face turned red. Henry, putting aside the grim events of this execution day, joined me in youthful laughter.

"That was close, Mister Slick!" he chortled.

"Close?" I said. "That was more than close, young fella. I swear I saw the gates of Hell open to meet me."

The humour left my face for a moment. "Thank you, Henry Appleton," I said. "Thank you most sincerely. You have saved the life of this wretched scribe. I cannot wait to tell Wild Bill. To tell him all about my narrow escape from the jaws o' death."

I looked at the muddy condition of the two of us, and guffawed.

"If only Wild Bill could see us now!" I said.

Henry grinned. "Yes," he said, "if only Wild Bill could see us now."

THE END

POSTSCRIPT
WAS BURGESS REALLY HENRY'S FATHER?

Having enjoyed reading young Henry's adventures, you may now be asking yourself: how likely is that Richard Burgess, real name Richard Hill, was actually Henry Appleton's father, as he claimed?

In the humble opinion of this writer, and risking ridicule, the answer is yes.

We know that Henry was born in England in 1851, and it is a matter of public record that Burgess was transported from England to Australia several years earlier – in 1847. Ergo, he was on the other side of the world when Henry was conceived. Victoria Appleton and her son Henry did not know this or they would have challenged Burgess's claims of fatherhood.

But why would Burgess make up such a fanciful story, when there was no profit in it? It seems to this writer that Burgess genuinely believed he was Henry's father, and had gone to some lengths to obtain the birth records to support his case.

In the course of his investigations, this writer heard a rumour, which has never been substantiated, that Burgess returned to England around 1848 and lived there for several years. This means he could well have been in the same city as Henry's birth mother at the time of Henry's conception.

It may seem preposterous that this notorious criminal Richard Burgess, with his distinctive appearance, well known to police and prison authorities, could somehow smuggle himself aboard a ship bound for England. Indeed, there is no record of such a trip, and no record of a Richard Hill or Richard Burgess being arrested in England and returned to Australia.

To succeed in such a venture, Burgess would have had to disguise his appearance on a journey of some three months in order to step foot in England without being arrested at the docks.

This writer believes this scenario is possible.

Admittedly there is no record of Burgess using disguises, but why would there be? And he was an intelligent, devious and inventive man, quite capable of such a grand piece of subterfuge.

Most observers insist that Henry Appleton was

hoodwinked by a plausible yet evil career criminal; that it was only thanks to his upbringing by the good William and Victoria Appleton, and the intervention of the physician Zephaniah Smith, that Henry was not forever condemned to a miserable life through Burgess's odious inventions.

This writer chooses to leave open the possibility that Burgess was Henry's father. However, one is obliged to ask: does it matter? The most important point, and one to celebrate, is that Doctor Henry Appleton chose a path in life that was in complete contrast to the path chosen by Richard Burgess, whether Burgess was his father or not.

This is a photo of W.H. West's Saloon and Tobacconist in Hardy Street, where Henry Appleton confronted the bank robbers and was shot at. (*Photo by courtesy of Nelson Provincial Museum, Davis Collection: 10279*)

REFERENCES AND FURTHER READING

Suggestions from John Evan Harris, author of The Physician's Gun

EARLY NEWSPAPERS and other ONLINE RESOURCES

Old newspapers are a fantastic way to learn more about Nelson in the 1800s, in the language of the time.

Nelson newspapers – the *Nelson Examiner, The Colonist, Nelson Evening Mail.* (www.paperspast.natlib.govt.nz).

Stevens and Bartholomew's New Zealand directory for 1866–67, available from the National Library (https://natlib.govt.nz/records/20602794) among many other libraries, contains a list of inhabitants of Nelson and their occupations. A wonderful insight into the makeup of Nelson's community in the days of *Henry Appleton, Boy Hero* and *The Physician's Gun.*

The Prow (www.theprow.org.nz), a website featuring historical and cultural stories from Nelson, Tasman and Marlborough, is a wonderful resource for researchers and teachers. It's a collaboration between the Nelson City, Tasman and Marlborough District Libraries, Nelson Marlborough Institute of Technology and The Nelson Provincial Museum, and among its treasures are the digitized journals of the Nelson Historical Society.

REFERENCE BOOKS

There are many books available in your local library – a few of which I have read, and acknowledge:

'**The Nelson Police – The story of the Nelson Police District 1841–1986**' by June E. Neale.

'**Te Tau Ihu o Te Waka: A history of Māori of Nelson and Marlborough, Volume II: Te Ara Hou – The New Society**' by Hilary and John Mitchell (Huia Publishers in association with Wakatū Incorporation.) This is an exhaustively researched and referenced book with first-hand accounts by early European settlers, and many illustrations.

- The conflict between traditional Māori beliefs and Christianity: Page 124
- A European's description of a pā and the Māori way of life: Page 155
- A description of urupā (burial sites) including pictures of upright monuments: Page 439–442

'**Nelson – A history of early settlement**' by Ruth M. Allan (A H & A W Reed 1965), available through the Nelson Provincial Museum. This impressively-detailed book mainly concerns the 1839–1844 period, although some parts go up to the 1850s. It has a great deal of well-researched facts about the New Zealand Company, NZ-UK politics, the governors/company agents, land dealings. Also: The Wairau Incident / Massacre / Affray of 1843.

'**Diggers Hatters & Whores**': The story of the NZ Gold Rushes by Stevan Eldred-Grigg (Random House New Zealand, 2008)

'**Working away, unseen: stories of the lives of Nelson women**' by STEM Writers of Nelson (STEM Writers, 2019)

'**Colonial Experiences in New Zealand**' by 'An Old Colonist', believed to be William Pratt. (Chapman Hall, 1877.)

'Exotic Intruders' by Joan Druett (Heinemann, 1983), part of the Victoria University of Wellington Library's online New Zealand Texts Collection: a description of the trees and plants encountered by early European settlers.

'Birdstories: a history of the birds of New Zealand', by Geoff Norman (Potton and Burton, Nelson 2018.) A wonderfully illustrated book where it's fun to learn the Māori words for Aotearoa's huge range of birds: the kākāriki, pīwakawaka, tūi, kererū, korimako, pītoitoi, kōtare, kakaruwai, piopio, pīpīwharauroa, pīhoihoi, tītitipounamu, pīwauwau, pihipihi, hihi, riroriro...

'Ngā Waka Māori: Māori Canoes' by Anne Nelson (Macmillan Co of New Zealand, 1991).

'Handguns and Police in New Zealand 1840–1990' by John Osborne (South Pacific Armoury, 1990).

THE WORLD OF JOHNNY SLICK

If you're interested in the American dime novel author Johnny Slick, you might research the writers of other early dime novels, or the outlaws who featured in their wildly-popular books.

'Dime Novel Desperadoes: the notorious Maxwell Brothers', by John E Hallwas (University of Illinois Press 2011).

Or why not read one of the many books written by Ned Buntline (real name Colonel E. Z. C. Judson), the American writer who inspired Johnny Slick:

'Buffalo Bill and his adventures in the West' by Ned Buntline (J. S. Ogilvie and Company, New York 1886), reprinted in 2006 by Stonecrest Industries (www.stonecrestindustries.com).

'**Wild Bill's Last Trail**' by Ned Buntline (Dodo Press).

* * *

For more background information, visit John Evan Harris' author
website:
www.johnevanharris.com

WORTH A VISIT

If you're lucky enough to live in – or visit – Nelson, there are many places where you can 'experience' history:

The Nelson Provincial Museum (www.nelsonmu seum.co.nz) is in the centre of town at the corner of Trafalgar and Hardy Streets. It contains a wealth of exhibits from early Nelson – and specifically, a section on the Burgess Gang. Here you can see the plaster cast 'death masks' of the three hanged men, featured in *The Physician's Gun*, plus fascinating items such as Burgess's crucifix-shaped document.

Nelson Cathedral (www.nelsoncathedral.org) is a magnificent building which sits on the hill known as Pikimai, which translates as 'climb hither'. The hill has a commanding view of the town and the NZ Company quickly set up camp here. After the Wairau incident in which several prominent Nelson leaders died, fearful townsfolk built a redoubt here and named it Fort Arthur. Later there was parish church here (built in 1851) which Richard Burgess and his gang couldn't have failed to see, as it dominated the main street, although they probably didn't visit it. The cathedral wasn't built until more than 60 years after the Burgess gang terrified the town, but there are many reminders of turbulent earlier times including a wall plaque which reads simply "In Memory of those who fell at the Wairau, 17th of June 1843."

Isel House (www.nelson.govt.nz/iselhouse), off the main road, Stoke, was constructed by the Marsden family in the 1840s and onwards, using local stone. It contains old furniture and paintings and is surrounded by a woodland of heritage trees.

Broadgreen Historic House (www.nelson.govt.nz/broadgreen) is at 276 Nayland Road, Stoke. Built in 1855, it contains a collection of garments and everyday items, and boasts a magnificent garden which includes roses and other flowers and trees planted by early European settlers.

Founders Heritage Park (founderspark.co.nz) at 87 Atawhai Drive contains well-maintained houses, church and workshops and offices of the time including a replica of the Nelson Evening Mail newspaper office.

The restored Duncan House has information and pictures relating to the ill-fated New Zealand Company. There are sketches of notable Māori and European men and women of the 1800s plus information on Edward Gibbon Wakefield and his Nelson Settlement dream.

Wakapuaka cemetery is a picturesque and well-maintained historic site which contains the graves of many early settlers plus the monument to the memory of the victims of the Burgess gang. (www.nelson.govt. nz/services/facilities/cemeteries/cemeteries-in-nelson-2/wakapuaka-cemetery)

The South Street Heritage Precinct off Nile Street, is New Zealand's oldest fully-preserved street, where you can see modest but well-preserved cottages built for renting to local tradesmen in the 1860s.

ALSO BY JOHN EVAN HARRIS
THE PHYSICIAN'S GUN

Inspired by the notorious Maungatapu Murders of 1866, this action-packed historical novel is a gripping tale of murder and greed. Fifteen-year-old Henry Appleton devours American cowboy novels, and dreams of having his own rifle and becoming a gunslinger like Wild Bill Hickok. But his daydreaming becomes a terrifying reality with the arrival of the ruthless highwayman Richard Burgess.

"A lively yarn, with plenty of jeopardies and hair's-breadth escapes, which will appeal strongly to young males." — Trevor Agnew, *Magpies* magazine

"... has the action that many young people want in a modern novel". Highly Recommended.

— Chris Reed , *Read NZ Te Pou Muramura*